garden of

THORNS

USA TODAY BESTSELLING AUTHOR

KEARY TAYLOR

also by
KEARY TAYLOR

The House Of Royals Series

The Fall Of Angels Trilogy

The Eden Trilogy

The Mccain Saga

What I Didn't Say

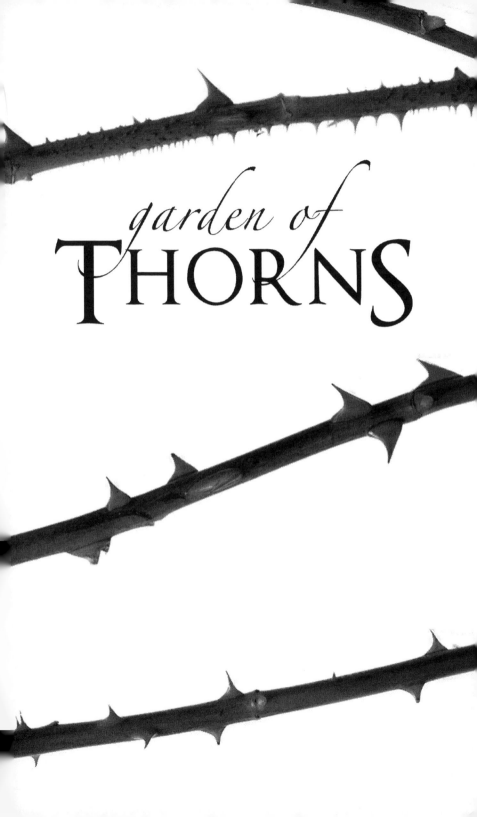

garden of
THORNS

"I T WILL ALL BE OVER in a few hours," I say, staring into his yellow eyes. I take half a step back as he lunges toward me, his lengthened fangs snapping in my face.

Kai tightens his grip on the man in the dirty and torn clothes, yanking him away from me. His own yellow eyes flash, igniting brilliantly as his enhanced muscles flex against the struggling Bitten.

"I'm so sorry," the man hisses. "I can't… I swear I'm trying to control it."

"I know," I say calmly as I turn away from him. I walk across the dimly lit room to the seemingly mundane wall. I lift the ugly painting of the ashy sky over a decaying barn and swing it on hinges away from the wall, revealing a keypad hidden beneath. I punch in the pin code and the wall unlocks. I slide it open, revealing a small, glass-faced refrigerator. I open it, taking out a vial of amber-colored liquid.

"It's a single injection," I explain as I slide the wall closed and open the other side. A cabinet reveals phlebotomy supplies. I take what I need, and close the wall once more. It automatically locks. "It's going to hurt, a lot, for about a minute. You'll pass out, and then you'll sleep for about a day while the toxins burn out of your system. When you wake up, you'll be back to normal."

"Thank you," he says. I turn to see him squeeze his eyes closed, forcing a stream of tears down his face.

Kai tightens his grip as I walk closer and the man snaps his teeth at me once more. He locks his enormous hand over the man's face, holding his fangs away from me as I pull his sleeve up and sink the needle into his skin.

The miracle created by a man over six hundred years old rushes into the blood of a being created by mistake. I pull the needle from his body and take a step back.

He howls in pain, a fierce roar that rips from his throat. He throws his head back, every single muscle in his body tensing. His eyes fly open, brilliant and yellow.

A moment later he curls in on himself, collapsing to the concrete floor as Kai releases him. It's as if he is crumpling inward, becoming smaller and smaller as he tries to contain the pain slashing through his body. His breath rips in and out between clenched teeth.

The shaking takes over for about twenty seconds. But slowly, it calms. He stills. His breathing becomes slower.

And he collapses to the hard floor.

"Let's move him to the bed," I say, disposing of the empty vial and needle into the sharps container.

"I really thought that one was going to bite you," Kai says as he scoops his arms under the man and easily lifts him. He takes half a dozen steps to the cot that sits in a corner and lays the man on it, his head resting on the pillow. "I'm sorry. He was much stronger than he looked."

"You did fine," I say, though, instinctually, I pull my sleeves further down my arms, covering the myriad of white scars there. "You always do."

Kai doesn't say anything, and I know he's disappointed in the work he's done. He's always so hard on himself.

I look down at the watch on my wrist. "It's 9:32 PM," I say to myself. "He'll probably wake up around nine tomorrow night. Let's just make sure he can find the note when he wakes up."

But I don't even have to tell Kai. He already has a white envelope in his hand and a roll of tape in the other. He sets the envelope on the back of the man's hand, stretching back over his wrist, and takes the tape, winding it around it twice so it won't fall off.

Inside the envelope are instructions to take the same door he entered through, walk down the hallway and then follow the steps up to the alley behind the row of buildings here. He's to exit onto the road to the south.

And not look back.

To never mention this place again, unless it's to another Bitten in need.

I double-check that everything is securely locked up. Most especially that the motion sensor for the back door is on, the one that turns on a light upstairs, letting me know I've got company.

"Let's go."

My footsteps echo as I follow Kai down the dark hallway. Moisture and history trigger all kinds of smells. It stretches for two-dozen yards before leading up a set of stairs. We take them and at the top I enter another pin code, opening yet another hidden door.

Dim light barely grants enough to see by as I lock the door behind me.

"You ready?" Kai asks, waiting by the door. He looks out the windows, always searching for danger and threats.

"Yeah," I breathe, the exhaustion finally hitting me. I look around the space one last time, making sure I haven't forgotten anything.

Shelves line two walls, filled to the max with glass bottles, vials, satchels and other unexpected things. A counter sits before the third wall where customers check out or come for consultations.

It smells of spices and herbs and cures.

A smile cracks in one corner of my lips as I look around.

This is home.

My sanctuary.

"Let's go," Kai says as he opens the door.

I lock the shop behind me and the two of us take off down the road.

We pass dozens of other shops and restaurants, all closed at this very late hour, cutting through the park, and then down a street packed with dozens and dozens of Victorian brownstones. My home sits only a fifteen-minute walk from Oleander Apothecary.

"You want me to come in?" Kai asks, looking to the front door, same as he does every night.

"I'm sure I'll be fine," I say, offering him a smile.

"Goodnight then," he says as he presses a kiss to the top of my head.

I look back once as I walk up the steps to the front door. It's already difficult to find him in the dark, his chocolate skin and black tattoos blending him into the dark night. He nods once to me as I wave goodbye and step inside.

I walk up two flights of stairs before unlocking the door to my own apartment. Shada immediately runs over to my feet, even as I'm tripping over her, and starts rubbing her head over my legs. I stoop down and scoop up the black cat, scratching behind her warm ears with my frozen fingers as I walk back toward the kitchen.

"Did you miss me today?" I purr to her absentmindedly as I pull some leftovers from dinner the other night and put them in the microwave. She paws at me for a moment and then hisses, her signal to be put down. I watch with a smile as she darts out of the kitchen and around the corner.

The front door leads straight into the small living room. A fireplace occupies one of the walls, wooden baseboards and paneling running beautifully throughout the house. It leads back into a good-sized kitchen with a dining room off to the side of it. From the living room rises a set of stairs, the same beautiful wood panels framing them in. At the top of the stairs is a master bedroom, a spare bedroom, a bathroom, and a laundry room with stairs leading up to the rooftop garden.

I occupy the Victorian brownstone all by myself, as I have for the past year and a half.

I've never been one to be bothered by being by myself. For two years I lived in a crowded house with twenty people in it, but before that it was just my family. The three of us. And now it's just me.

And Kai sometimes.

Exhausted from the long day, I take my food and after locking the doors, I head up to my bedroom. The clock on the dresser reads eleven-thirty.

I've barely sat down on my bed when there's a loud knock on the front door.

"Elle!" I hear Kai yell from out on the landing. "You got a visitor."

My pulse spikes and I dart from my room, down the stairs, to the door, where Shada is hiding behind a chair, hissing.

I yank it open.

Kai has his huge hands fisted in the jacket of a man whose eyes glow brilliant red.

"Ian?"

chapter
TWO

"WHAT ARE YOU DOING HERE?" I demand, folding my arms over my chest. "Kai, it's okay, let him go. This is my brother, Ian."

Kai looks from me to Ian, doubt in his protective eyes. Ian glares death at the much larger man, and I can tell, my brother is using everything he has in him not to rip Kai apart.

"What are both of you doing here?" I ask, turning my eyes on Kai. "You were supposed to go home."

"There was a smell in the air," he says, eying my brother up and down.

"Did he just say I stink?" Ian asks, cocking an eyebrow and stepping forward. I step aside, letting him in.

"All the Born stink," Kai says, following Ian inside, even though he wasn't invited.

"Elle, who is this?" Ian demands, his brows furrowed as he takes a step toward Kai, his eyes flashing.

"Just stop," I say, holding a hand up and pushing on his chest to make him back up. "Ian, this is Kai Ioane, my friend."

"You frequently make friends with Bitten?" Ian hisses. And I can't blame him. Not after everything we've been through. Especially him.

"You got a problem with us, stop making us," Kai hisses, taking a step forward, the muscles in his huge arms flexing.

"Kai," I glower, turning serious eyes on him. "Seriously, don't go pissing my brother off. I'm perfectly safe and it won't end well for you if he thinks you're threatening me."

"Safe," Ian says. "Kind of hard to be safe around them until they're cured."

"I'm the only one who keeps her safe!" Kai yells, his Samoan temper flaring. "You're the one who puts her in danger with your very name!"

"Will both of you just stop it!" I yell, stepping between them again, my hands up to keep them apart. As if I could begin to stop them if they decided to fight. "Ian, sit down." I point to the chair next to the fireplace. "You too." I direct Kai to take a seat on the stairs, as far apart as I can get them. "Now if both of you will stop acting like heathens, I'll introduce and explain."

The heat in their eyes doesn't die right away and the curl of their fingers doesn't relax. But finally, Kai sits on the steps. A moment later, Ian also sinks into the chair.

"I don't think my brother requires much introduction, you've already heard a lot about him," I say to Kai. "This is Ian. He still lives in Mississippi with my sister-in-law, Alivia. They run the House that covers the whole South East part of the States."

Kai nods, having heard all of this information before.

"Ian, this is Kai Ioane," I say, turning to my hot head brother. "He's my…"

"Body guard," he fills in when I can't quite come up with an explanation for our relationship.

"Really?" Ian cocks an eyebrow at me, his expression disbelieving.

"Really," I spit back, annoyed.

"What happened to Terra?" Ian asks. "That's the whole reason I sent her up, to help you and keep you safe."

"She drew too much attention," I say, shaking my head. "She might not have had any House affiliations, but she could still be traced back to you. Plus, we didn't get along so well."

Understatement.

"How long ago did you send her away?" Ian asks, ever annoyed by *everything*.

Sometimes I don't know how Liv can stand to be married to my brother.

"About nine months ago," I answer quietly, because I know he won't be happy.

"What?!" he explodes, exactly as I expected.

"Look, I ran into Kai just a week later," I rush on to explain. "I actually killed the Born who turned him."

Kai nods. "It's true. She found us in an alley just a few blocks from here, my cousin and I. The Born had finished me off, or nearly did. She'd moved on to my cousin, Lecka. Elle shot her with that toxin and had to stake her."

"I brought Kai back to the shop," I explain. "I've never seen control like his, Ian. He feeds, but he's never been out of control."

"When she explained what she does, I offered to help protect her," Kai says. "It was clear pretty fast she was always putting herself in danger."

Ian's keen eyes instantly jump to my right wrist where my sleeve has worked its way up a bit, exposing the white scars there.

"He's been helping me ever since," I say, looking back at my friend.

Kai is my total opposite in every physical way. I'm only about five foot four, he's about six foot two. His dark, Samoan skin is covered in all kinds of tribal tattoos. Heavily banded in muscle. His dark, curly hair hangs down his back, tied at the back of his head. A wide nose, an upper lip that is slightly thicker than his lower, and deep soulful eyes balance out a beautiful, handsome face.

But it's not like that.

Kai is my friend.

"You deal with his kind all the time," Ian says, his eyes never leaving Kai. "You've been there for everything Cora put us through. And you trust him?"

I look away from my brother to my friend, who returns my gaze. "I do."

Ian makes a little sound and looks away with the shake of his head.

I sigh. The last few years have brought about so much change, but so much anger and resentment and discrimination.

And death.

"Kai, you should go home," I say. I rub my eyes, probably messing up my makeup, but I'm too tired to care.

He shakes his head. "No."

"I'm not just making a suggestion," I say, trying to plead with him with my eyes. "I'm fine. I will see you tomorrow. Please. I'm tired."

Kai looks from me to my brother. I can see in his eyes that this is killing him. But he will do anything I ask.

Finally, he rises and goes to the door. "Call me if you need me. For anything."

I nod. "I will."

He closes the door behind him. But I feel Ian bristle all the harder behind me.

"I don't want you to say a word," I assert. I turn to face Ian. "Kai has never made me feel like I'm in danger. He's done nothing but protect and help me. I'm not going to send him away, and you're not going to kill him."

The look in Ian's eyes tells me he'd thought about it. It may have been years since my brother was a vampire hunter, but those instincts surely haven't gone away.

"Now," I say. "How about you come upstairs with me, where my dinner was interrupted, and we can talk."

I study my brother. I've memorized his face my entire life. And even though it's been a year and a half since I've seen him, nearly five years since I lived with him, not a line or detail to his face has changed. Not for the last seven years.

"Okay," he finally agrees.

"Everything's been okay here?" Ian asks as he paces my bedroom. He twirls a stake between his fingers; a habit that I don't think is ever going to go away. "Especially in the last few weeks?"

"Things have been normal," I say with a nod, taking another bite of my leftovers. I chew it, watching my brother. I recognize all the signs. The lines that tighten around his eyes, the way his lips thin out. The fact that the stake is spinning so fast now that I can't see anything more than a blur.

Something is wrong.

"What is it?"

He suddenly snaps the stake into his hand, stilling it instantly. He stands there with his hands on his hips for a second, breathing hard, angry.

"I think you should move back down South," he says. He doesn't look in my direction when he does, because he, too, knows me well.

"Not necessarily to Mississippi. Just back into Conrath territory."

"You have to tell me why." I swallow past the rock that's forming in my throat and push the frustration and anxiety away.

It's what I do.

Ian finally looks over at me. His lips tighten all the further and his eyes are narrowed. The knuckles of the hand that holds the stake have turned white.

"There are rumors going around that King Cyrus is sending spies and hunters to fully enact the Bitten eradication order." My brother shifts from one foot to the other, never able to hold still when he's agitated, and that's most of the time. "I think there's going to be an investigation at each House, an inquiry of all the members, looking for leads on Bitten."

"So what does that have to do with me moving back into Conrath territory?" I question, setting my plate aside, my dinner finished. "If anything, that's worse. It brings my work closer to the danger area."

Ian shakes his head. "Because Charles Allaway has been making threats. He's been acting erratically, more so than normal. He hates the Bitten, a hundred times more so after what happened to his sister. I'm worried he might know something about Henry's cure. He's been talking shit to the other Royals about Liv, about the entire Conrath House. You're in danger because of this family, Elle."

"Charles Allaway," I say, the name sticking on my tongue. It's one I haven't thought about in years. "Why is he suddenly popping up?"

Ian shakes his head. "He's hated us ever since his sister was murdered six years ago, but he's been fairly docile until recently. There has to be a reason he's jumping to action now."

Six years ago, Charles and his twin sister Chelsea came to Silent Bend, invited by King Cyrus to Alivia's introduction party. Cyrus had his fun, tortured both the Houses by making them trade members, causing quite the stir. When the Allaways left that night, almost all of their members were slaughtered just down the road from Alivia's house. Including Chelsea.

They were killed by an army of Bitten, led by my own mother, Cora Ward.

"Ian, I can't just pack up and leave," I say, studying him. He's looking everywhere but at me. "I have a life here in Boston. I have my shop, I own this house. I love it here."

His eyes finally snap to me and I can see the familiar brotherly pleading in them. "Elle," he crosses the room to sit at the foot of the bed, sinking down on it. "You live in Allaway territory. Liv and I have no rights here, no power. If he finds out about you, he could come after you. I highly doubt that mountain of muscle can protect you against the entire House of Allaway."

"I've been careful, Ian," I say. The defenses are rising up inside of me. Once again, I feel like I'm sixteen years old, being bossed around by my big brother, who took guardianship over me for two years, but really raised me my entire life. But I'm twenty-two now, about to turn twenty-three. I take care of myself. "The Bitten never come to my house. When they come to see me it's through a back entrance, away from my shop. I don't even go by my real name here. To everyone except Kai, my name is Penny Jones."

"You don't understand how intense these people are who work for the King," Ian says with the shake of his head. "Most of them have hundreds of years of training. They're so invisible it might be months before you suspect they're there."

He turns to face me, begging me to agree to head back toward home. "I can't protect you here, Elle."

I reach out, taking one of his hands in mine. Looking into his eyes, I marvel how the eight and a half year age gap between us has almost been eliminated. To a stranger, we would probably look just about the same age. Though it is unlikely they would mistake us for siblings. We don't look much alike. We do have different fathers, after all.

"My work here is too important," I say quietly. "I've begun to establish a presence here, a reputation."

"And that puts you at risk," he interrupts me. "If any *Bitten* can find you now, so can Charles. So could Cyrus."

"And think how many innocent lives will be lost if I just pick up and leave?" I reason, begging him to really hear what I'm saying. "There are too many of them out there that need help, Ian."

"How long has it been since the last one came to you?" he asks.

"About two hours ago." I hold back the tiny satisfied smile that wants to break onto my lips.

And I see the defeat fall in his eyes. He lets them slide closed and falls onto his back on my bed. "I never should have let you and Henry talk me into letting you be the one to do this."

"You know there wasn't anyone else," I say, pushing his hair off of his forehead. He may be immortal now, Resurrected, and hasn't aged in six years, but the worry lines there had been carving their way into his forehead since he was ten years old.

Ian only lets out a sigh and reaches over to take my hand in his. He holds it over his heart, grasping on to me tightly.

After the insurgence my mother caused with her Army of Bitten, after the battle that claimed the life of some of Alivia's closest friends, the King of the vampires issued a decree.

The creation of any new Bitten was punishable by death. And he made it pretty clear that hunting them down and killing them would find anyone favor.

I was sixteen when that shift in the paranormal world happened.

So for two years, Alivia's father, Henry Conrath, who was once thought dead, came and went, taking with him the Bitten cure he'd developed for his best friend, Rath, who he'd turned once upon a time in order to save his life.

But the legend of Henry, the legend of the Conrath name was far too widespread and recent.

Henry was drawing too much attention. It put him, Alivia, Ian, the entire House in danger.

Henry came to me one night, just two weeks before I was to go to Northwestern University in Illinois. We had a long talk, one of the most fascinating and fulfilling in my eighteen years of life.

I'd been enthralled by botany and chemistry for as long as I could remember. I'd been creating my own concoctions for years; good enough the man himself had stolen several vials of my vampire toxin to study in his hidden lab.

I'd never considered Henry Conrath and I to have much in common until that night.

"You understand the science," he'd told me that night as we talked down by the Hanging Tree so as to not be overheard by my brother or Henry's daughter. "To everyone else in this House, it's essentially magic."

I smiled at that, because it was an entirely accurate description. Well, to those who actually knew about the Bitten cure.

"And there are very, very few of those in our world that even know of your existence," he continued, folding his hands behind his back as we stared out over the Mississippi River. "Your brother and my daughter have been very careful about that. You'll be nearly a thousand miles away from the House of Conrath. And me."

"You want me to help the Bitten?" I clarify.

"I want you to consider letting us, and others sympathetic to the cause, send deserving Bitten to you. And you administering the cure." He looked over at me, studying my reaction to his weighty request.

"Ian would never let me," I say with the shake of my head. "It would be dangerous for me, and you know how he is."

"I do," Henry said. "But he wouldn't have to know. At least not at first."

Henry Conrath always did things his own way, with his own skewed version of right and wrong.

Ian found out, a year later.

He very, *very* nearly killed Henry when everything came to light.

But he couldn't force me to stop—not when I'd already cured sixty-one innocent Bitten.

While other students at school were going to parties, getting drunk, and having sex, I was meeting vampires at seedy hotels, playing magician doctor, curing them of multi-millennia old science and a curse.

But there is a reason my body is covered in circular, white scars. A reason I always keep a second vial around my neck now, alongside my toxin, just in case one of them ever sinks it's fangs into me and doesn't stop in time.

I'm constantly in danger, but how am I supposed to be selfish and stop when to date I've saved over five hundred Bitten, not to mention the lives of their future possible victims when they couldn't control their thirst?

I never had a normal college experience, but I'm proud of how I still laid claim on my own life.

I completed my degree in botany with a minor in chemistry from Northwestern in just over two years, thanks to two brutal summer semesters in the mix. A spur of the moment graduation trip, the first travel I'd ever really done in my entire life, led me through Boston two years ago. I fell in love with the city. And never left.

"We could have found someone," Ian says, pulling me back to the present. "Trained someone else."

I shake my head, searching his hazel eyes while he studies the ceiling. "I like what I do, Ian. I love my life."

He finally looks back at me, and I see it in his eyes, he knows I do.

"We'll talk again after we see how things go tomorrow night," he says as he rolls forward. His phone dings in his pocket and he pulls it out to study the screen. I see Liv's name but don't catch what she says.

"What's happening tomorrow night?" I ask as he stands. He quickly responds before sliding his phone back into his pocket.

"We're going to talk to Charles Allaway and see if we can reason with him," Ian says, folding his arms over his chest. "Their numbers are still small. We'll get ugly if we have to. They've never had to fight for anything. We have."

"You're possibly going to war with the Allaways tomorrow night?" I ask in disbelief. "Ian, you guys have finally been able to live in relative peace for the past five years. Are you really going to blow that all up?"

"This is a world of politics and power, Elle, you know that," he says. His voice grows tired though, sinking into the center of the Earth. "He's threatening us. The House of Conrath is still so new, we can't afford to let some ginger bully make us look weak for at least another few decades."

A little chuckle actually puffs from my nose. I shake my head.

"Your world is so unbelievable," I say, shaking my head as I rub my eyes. "How… how is this even your real life?"

"I've been asking myself that question since I was ten," he half laughs, half scoffs.

"Did you at least bring enough bodies to make this a proper fight if it comes to that?"

Ian nods. "We left Nial in charge back home, and two others, just to hold the fort down. But everyone else is with us. They're all headed to Vermont right now."

Everyone else. I try to total the numbers up in my head, but I don't know how many members Alivia has gained and lost in the four and a half years since I lived in the House. It has to be at least twenty though.

"Any idea how many members the Allaways are back up to?" I ask. They'd had thirty at one point, until my mother's army slaughtered more than half of them.

Ian shakes his head. "Rumor has it they lost several members after the massacre to the House in Vegas, and he's having a hard time rebuilding. I don't think it will be that many."

I nod. My mind is racing, going over the implications to so many things my brother is planning.

I've been so removed for so long now. I was so engrained in that world for two years while I lived among them, the only human in a House full of twenty vampires. But I've been gone, detached. It's disorienting getting caught back up to speed.

"We're going to show up at his mansion tomorrow night," Ian explains. "He doesn't know we're coming. We'll talk. Figure this crap out. If everything goes well and he agrees to back off, I'm hoping to get word to you the day after tomorrow."

I nod, even as my resolve hardens. Ian may have plans to drag me back down South, but no matter the outcome, I'm staying.

But he doesn't need that on his mind right now.

"I hope it goes well," I say. I stand and head to the bathroom where I begin brushing my teeth. I feel my brother's eyes on me the whole time, always watching, always studying.

"It's been a long day, and it's nearly midnight," I say as I walk into the closet, half shutting the door, and changing into pajamas behind it. "I'm beat. And as much as I really would love to stay up half the night catching up, I don't think my eyes are going to stay open."

"Yeah," he says, going into guardian mode just like that. "You get some sleep. I can stay until morning."

Which translates to mean he's going to spend all night standing guard over me, just in case Charles Allaway suddenly gets wind of my location tonight and decides to come after me.

I smile as I climb under the covers and turn off the lamp. "Goodnight, Ian. I'm really glad you're here."

He smiles back, barely visible through the dark as he heads to the door. "Night, Elle."

chapter
FOUR

IAN LEFT AROUND SEVEN THE next morning. As I said goodbye to him on the front porch, I found Kai sitting on the curb across the street, wearing the same clothes he wore yesterday.

Ian gave me a look before heading to his rental car, one I wasn't quite sure said, *watch him like a hawk*, or *I'm glad at least someone is keeping an eye on you*.

Kai makes breakfast while I get dressed and ready for the day. Fall is quickly bringing a chill to the air, and having grown up in the South, I'm *always* freezing here, so I settle for black slacks and a long sleeved black and white turtleneck. I leave my platinum blonde hair hanging. My blue eyes practically glow as I look in the mirror.

"You have a nice reunion with your brother last night?" Kai asks as he sets a plate of *panikeke*, eggs, and bacon in front of me, way more food than I could ever finish off.

"I did," I respond, scooping a forkful of eggs. "Did you have a nice night out in the cold?"

"I did," he responds sarcastically.

"I bet your mother was worried sick when you didn't come home last night," I say as I eat quickly. I'm running late and I need to be to the shop in twenty minutes to open.

I've never actually met Kai's family. Meeting new people sometimes gives me anxiety. My world is so far removed from theirs, it's sometimes hard to relate. But Kai talks about his family members so much that I feel as if I know them.

"She called several times," he says as he sets the pans in the sink and fills it to soak them. He turns to his own food and starts eating. Or more like inhaling. "She's worried about you."

"Everyone needs to *stop* worrying about me," I sigh. It feels like that is the sum of my entire life. Everyone protecting and worrying about me. I've certainly felt loved, but you have to let a woman grow up eventually.

"She worries about everyone."

Kai's family moved to Boston from Samoa when Kai was only two. Kai's dad owns a landscape company and his two older brothers help him run it. Kai works with him when he isn't helping me. He and his two younger sisters still live with their parents.

They have no idea their son is a vampire. He keeps his cool and hunger under control so his eyes never flash yellow, and he only feeds on donated blood. With the aid of the contacts Henry continues to send me every other week, he's been able to go out during the day most of the time.

"We should get going," I say as I stuff the last bit of food I can possibly fit into my stomach. I scrape my plate clear and set it in the sink. Kai clears the rest away as I dart upstairs to collect the plants I need for the day.

I bought this place, not for the house, but for the rooftop. Real estate in Boston comes at a premium and there's not a whole lot of extra space, so the second the little brownstone condo with the private rooftop came on the market, I made an offer the same day, full price. While in college, I'd invested the money I inherited from Lula, as well as the money Ian gave me from the sale of her house. Business had been good in the first six months I'd opened Oleander Apothecary, and I was fortunate to buy my own place in Boston's prestigious and pricey Back Bay neighborhood.

I spent weeks constructing the garden boxes that sit stacked in neat rows, a dozen deep, a set on each side with an aisle running down the middle.

They're generally classified into two sections, one on each side: medicinal and poisonous.

I stoop at the gardening cart just to the side of the stairs and grab an oversized glass jar, gloves, and pruning sheers, and lastly a plastic baggie.

The morning air is thick with fog, cold and sticky. I'm going to have to put up the greenhouse covers before too long. I cut through the aisle, toward the back. Opening my bag, I snip some Evening Primrose, tuck them into my bag, and then move to the middle section of the other side of the yard.

I carefully pull on the gloves, making sure my wrists are covered up. Even brushing up against stinging nettle will cause fiery pain to shoot through my limbs. I snip just one branch off of the bush and slip it into the glass jar, screwing the lid on tight.

Ready to take off, I lock the apartment up behind me, and Kai and I head toward the shop.

A narrow park cuts through the center of Back Bay, plaques and sculptures scattered throughout it here and there, commemorating Boston's deep history. Beautiful Victorian brownstones line the street, one of the parts about the city that I love the most. You don't get buildings like this in the South.

We cut through the Boston Public Garden, and turn up the street into Beacon Hill. The streets are busy and packed the closer I get to the shop. No one meets each other's eye with a smile. Not a word of *hello* or *how you doing* like in Mississippi. People don't really talk to each other, and I wouldn't call New Englanders friendly. And I like it that way. I'm the kind of person who keeps to herself, and so is everyone else around me.

This neighborhood is a historical one, and attracts a lot of tourists. The business street runs right up the middle, and tightly packed Federal-style row houses are crammed in as tight as they can fit. I'm not sure which neighborhood, this one, or mine, is more enchanting.

Teresa Beck already stands anxiously outside the doors to *Oleander Apothecary*. She bounces on the balls of her feet, peering impatiently into the windows.

"Miss Beck," I say as I walk up, causing her to jump. "I open at eight AM, Monday through Friday. I promise you that isn't going to change."

"Hi, Penny. I was just hoping maybe you might be in a little early," she says, looking embarrassed, stepping aside so I can open the door. I barely get the lights on before she steps inside, hustling up to the counter. "I'm already out, and James was acting really annoyed with me, and I just started panicking I guess."

I hang my purse on its hook, not even noticing Kai as he takes a walk around the shop, stepping into the back room lab.

I walk to the shelf that lines the very back wall, the one that holds the custom orders. I grab a glass perfume bottle from the middle row and set it on the counter. I hold a light up to it, observing the milky pale pink contents.

"It should probably sit for one more day—"

"I'm sure it will be just fine now," she says with a laugh, grabbing the lid and jamming it back on the bottle, pulling it protectively to her chest. "That will be one-fifty, right?"

I sigh but nod. She hands me the cash and hastily shuffles out of the shop.

"Does that stuff really work?" Kai asks as he walks out of the lab.

"To some degree," I shrug. "Everything in that mixture is geared toward relaxation, happiness. The familiar scents should induce feelings of comfort and euphoria. The pheromones certainly have some effect. But half of it's mental, truthfully."

Out of everything in my shop, my *Adore Me* "love perfume" is the least scientifically based, the product I'm least confident in, but the one that sells the very best.

I also make custom batches of it, based on an individual's specific scent and hormone levels. Teresa has been buying mass amounts of it from me for the past six months while she tries to get this James character to marry her.

I'm sure it has nothing to do with the large amounts of money he makes.

"Everything look good?" I ask as I open the folder on the counter, which contains my schedule.

Kai nods with a little grunt. "I'll be back tonight to make sure the guy in the basement made his way out."

"You have your keys?"

He mumbles an affirmative. I look up as I hear him walking to the door. "Hey," I call out. He looks back, his eyes hopeful and ready for whatever I ask. "Thank you. I mean, it wasn't necessary, you staying around last night, but I appreciate it. It's nice to have someone who cares."

There's something weighty in his eyes when he offers me a small smile and a nod. He turns and walks out, headed to work for the day.

I sigh as the door swings closed and I watch him walk off.

My relationship with Kai is very simple. He's always around to some degree. I see him nearly every single day. He's the first person on my speed dial in case I need someone, and I swear, he's never more than a few minutes away.

Over the past few months I've come to suspect he has feelings for me that run deeper than friendship, though. He's never acted on them in any way outside the boundaries of our friendship, but it's just something

I can feel. He would like what is between us to be more.

But he's waiting for reciprocation from my end.

The problem is that I just don't feel the same way. I love Kai, because he's always there for me. But there's something missing. We don't talk, not like lovers should. Not like two people in love would. Not like I see Ian and Alivia do.

And there's no electric spark that shoots through the air when we're together.

Not that I really know what that is.

Having grown up in a town that associated my name with hunting in the dark and the sad tale of a baby who lost her parents, everyone pretty much avoided me. The boys never looked my way.

Not that I'd ever been interested in the same dozen boys from my class that I'd known since we were all in diapers.

There were very few fish in the sea in Silent Bend.

The bell above the door rings and an elderly woman hobbles in.

"I sure hope you can help me," she says. Her Boston accent is thick. Sometimes it's fairly easy to tell the natives with deep roots. "I've tried everything to get this rash to clear up and nothing has helped."

"Why don't you give this a try," I say, stepping from behind the counter and walking over to one of the shelves.

chapter
FIVE

SOME OF MY PRODUCTS ARE boring and mundane, like stuff that clears up rashes. The tea that clears up any cold within two days, or the lavender oil that calms people down.

But then I get to pull out the lab equipment and deal with the deadly plants.

Nightshade is the basis for my vampire toxin. Along with a mix of other plants and chemistry, it's done the job of taking down any vampire, Born or Bitten, putting them through twelve hours of intense pain and inability to move.

I pull the microscope closer, peering down at the slides.

The cells from a Born are fascinating to study. They reproduce and replicate at astonishing rates. Like, a thousand times faster than a human's. And they don't look the same. It's a little more like a fossilized cell.

But the Bitten are entirely different. Their cells replicate and reproduce just like a human's. They're just … stronger.

The poor Bitten. They never stood a chance against the Born.

The Born are so much … more than the Bitten.

I pull out new petri dishes, scraping cells into each, one for the Born, one for the Bitten.

So far I've tested oleander and water hemlock. I've been trying to find anything that will affect the Born, but not the Bitten.

Unfortunately, that's working backwards. Trying to find something that harms the stronger of the two, but not the weaker.

Turning to the vials on a shelf, I pull out the white snakeroot. With a dropper, I suck up just a tiny amount. Dripping just a tiny amount onto each set of cells, I move them back under the microscope.

The cells of the Born are completely unaffected. No changes, no reaction whatsoever.

The cells of the Bitten have contracted somewhat, but other than that, no reaction.

White snakeroot would cause the Bitten some pain, but that's about it.

I'm not surprised, when it comes to supernatural uses, snakeroot is fairly useless.

I lean back in my chair, closer to the space heater running full blast, propping my feet up on the table. It's a problem I've been working on for six months now, and one I have yet to find a solution to, if there even is one.

My eyes wander around the lab that sits at the back of my shop. Counters line all four walls, shelves stacked above them. A row of refrigerators sit beneath the counter to my left. Vials and beakers wait in boxes. Slides and burners. A huge table in the middle of the space for working.

I've got a massive loan from the House of Conrath backing the cost of everything in this space.

It's not quite as impressive as Henry's lab, but it's not too shabby.

The computer that sits in one corner dings and I walk over to open the new email that pops up.

My skin rises with goosebumps when I see it's from Ruby Salazar.

Miss Jones, please make me up another batch. This time increase the citronella. I'll be in to pick it up just before you close.

A shiver works its way through my body as I click from this new email to the first she sent me two weeks ago.

Ruby contacted me, asking me to make a very specific oil she called Van Van Oil. She listed out all the ingredients, though there were no measurements. She described the consistency and the general process, the rest I had to figure out on my own. But she was offering to pay over a thousand dollars per bottle if I got it right.

I quickly dart out into the shop to be sure no one is waiting to be helped, before ducking back into lab. Pulling all the ingredients out, I fight off the shiver that wants to run down my spine once more.

I did some research once as to what Van Van Oil was. Words like hoodoo, voodoo, wiccan, and pagan came popping up all over the place. The info wasn't necessarily clear cut, as far as I could tell there were many things the oil was used for. Sometimes it was the basis for other oils. But other sources claimed it was used for clearing evil spirits, purification, protection, good luck.

It gave me the creeps making it.

I had hoped it would be a one and done deal.

Until just a few minutes ago.

But the money is impossible to ignore.

I scurry around the lab, gathering the ingredients I need: lemongrass, citronella, vetivert, palmarosa, lemon verbena, and lastly ginger grass.

Half of them aren't plants I work with on a regular basis, and it took me a week last time to gather everything. But with enough leftovers from the first go around, I'm ready to roll.

Mixing all the ingredients together, I pour them into a beaker and set it over a burner. Slowly, I turn up the heat, and wait for a minute until it all begins to simmer.

Over the next hour, the concoction slowly begins turning black.

Removing it from the heat, I drop in just one tiny drop of vetiver. The entire bottle instantly turns perfectly clear.

I swirl it around, watching its oily consistency stick to the side of the beaker.

Every now and then I get strange, custom requests. And usually I can somewhat figure out the scientific basis for what they're going after.

But Van Van Oil escapes me.

I set the beaker aside, letting it cool before I transfer it to a bottle.

A customer comes in while I wait and for the next six hours it's a steady flow of people coming in and out.

I've been in business for almost two years. I've never been against modern medicine, far from it. But the chemistry behind it all fascinated me. I wanted to learn my own methods. And I knew the capabilities of the plants I grew, and the ones I yearned to get my hands on and give a try.

I loved the experimentation of it all.

For me, opening the apothecary was a natural step and a dream come true. I loved experimenting and creating things that I knew worked, but seeing them work for others too? Incredibly satisfying.

Most of my customers are regulars. They came to me when they either couldn't afford the things they were prescribed, or they couldn't find anything that quite fit the bill. Or they were scared of doctors and pharmacies.

I'm out of the ordinary.

Something from a different time.

Tourists occasionally wander in, always smiling and ogling over the old wooden shelves filled with glass bottles and custom labels. They buy things as gag gifts for others, unaware that they are scientifically based and that I put my heart and soul into their development.

The tourists aren't my favorites.

But they do help pay the bills.

Mr. Peterson walks out with his remedy for insomnia, a satisfied smile on his face, just as the tall woman with the perfect hair steps inside.

"Ruby," I say, the name escaping my lips in a breath. "Hi."

She gives a little smile, her lips curling in a sinister way. She gets under my skin and she knows it. I get the impression she's the type of person who enjoys making people uncomfortable.

She's about five foot ten, slender and athletic. She wears black leather pants and always some kind of elaborately layered top. Her dark hair is always set in perfect waves, framing a beautiful but intimidating face.

"Hello, Miss Jones," she says as she stops in front of the counter. "Were you able to complete my order?"

"Of…of course," I say, barely managing to not squeak. "Just one second and I'll go get it for you."

I duck into the lab, glad to have the break from her for a moment.

She's probably only a year or two older than me, but everything about her sets me on edge. Like a cloud of electricity and ferocious wind follows her wherever she goes.

I handwrite Van Van Oil on the label before rolling it onto the bottle. It's a big one, sixteen entire ounces of it.

I walk back out, setting the bottle on the counter. She grabs it, pulls the cork, and takes a deep inhale. The scent of lemongrass drifts through the air, clean and crisp smelling.

"Perfect," she says with a smile, looking hard and deep at me. Like she can see straight through my skin.

"Would you like to pay with cash or a card?" I ask as my hands fumble at the register.

"I would have expected you to ask me what this stuff is for," Ruby says as she pulls a wallet from her purse and produces a card. "I get the impression this isn't the kind of custom order you get often."

"It's not," I say as I ring her up. "And sometimes I've found it's better to just not know."

I hand her card back to her, and she pulls that smile again.

"Fair enough," she responds as she puts her card away and carefully slips the bottle into her bag. She starts walking back to the door. "You walk to and from work, right?"

I swallow once. I don't know how she would know that. "Yes."

"Don't take too long," she says as she pulls the door open, looking back at me just once. "It's going to rain here in just a little bit."

She walks out without another word.

Slowly, I cross the shop, just as the grandfather clock chimes five o'clock. I gaze out the window, watching as Ruby walks down the road a little way to a black car that is parked on the side of the street. I can faintly make out the shape of two other women in it before they pull away and head down the road.

A brilliantly sunny day shows traces of only a few white and fluffy clouds.

I turn the sign on the door over to CLOSED and walk back into the lab. Carefully, I put all the vials and bottles back in their place, cleaning out the beakers and vials I used throughout the day.

Not the most productive day in the lab, but a good day in sales.

I grab my coat from the hook, pulling the strap of my bag over my shoulder. I pull out my phone to text Ian as I head for the door. When I look up to step outside and lock the doors, I freeze.

The skies that were blue and sunny just a few minutes ago are now dark, heavy and threatening clouds hanging over Boston.

I hurry out, locking the door securely behind me.

Everything going okay so far? I text my brother. Just as I hit send, a fat raindrop lands on my screen.

I pick up my pace, looking up as the sky continues to darken.

I've seen some weird stuff. Dead trees in the middle of Silent Bend where an innocent man was hung. A swamp that was once a producing cotton plantation. A storm that was centered directly over my hometown with swirling clouds and freezing temperatures that brought six-foot deep snow.

So this sky kind of freaks me out a little bit.

I'm just a block away from home when my phone dings, and my heart jumps a little higher in my chest. But I find a text from Kai instead of Ian.

Getting stuff ready for what looks like a bad storm. Working late. You good?

I shake my head, even as a tiny smile comes to my lips. *I'm good. Stay dry. Let me know if there are any problems with the patient tonight. See you tomorrow.*

Will do.

I check my messages again, but no response from Ian.

The rain starts pounding just as I run up the steps to my place. I'm half drenched by the time I dart through the front door.

I pull open the drawer in the kitchen that contains the takeout menus. Lula taught me to cook everything under the sun, and I spent the last year of her life cooking her endless meals, because she never ate anything that wasn't homemade. I have skills when it comes to the kitchen.

But I can't say I like to cook. Certainly not for just one person.

As I order some Chinese, I wonder for the thousandth time if I should get a housemate. A little company might be nice now and then.

But when I shower and climb out, checking my phone immediately out of habit, I remember the reality of what my world is really like.

Ran into an innocent on the way to VT today. Sent her your way. Will probably be there in the morning, early.

Henry.

It happens pretty frequently. I get heads-up texts, letting me know he's met some Bitten who needs my help.

I never ask them questions. I purposefully don't even try to get their names and don't tell them mine, because that creates connections that can be traced back to me, and I do have to be careful.

But I always wonder how they're actually able to get to me.

When a vampire turns someone into a Bitten, whether on accident or on purpose, a link is created called the Debt. That Bitten will do anything the other vampire says and won't be able to fight the command. They'd murder their own sister if they were told to do so by their sire.

They also generally have an insatiable pull to be close to their sire. Alivia accidently created one when she was first Resurrected, and the poor girl woke up alone, no idea what she was. But she had this irresistible urge to search for someone she didn't even know. She looked, until she finally found Alivia.

I know most of the Bitten who come to me travel some distance. How they're able to leave is a testament to how much they want to be free of the life most of them didn't ask for.

Got it, I text Henry back. *I'll be there before sunrise.*

My food arrives and I curl onto the couch to read while I eat. But I can't focus. I keep checking my phone every few minutes, silently willing Ian to text back.

It's dark outside now. I can feel the countdown ticking down to when my brother walks up the stairs to Charles' front door.

I know my brother. Know he doesn't often settle ordeals without getting physical.

I know Alivia. How when push comes to shove, she doesn't back down, even if the enemy is bigger than she is.

I know how loyal those House members are to her, and how they'll do anything she asks.

I jump hard when my phone vibrates from the coffee table. My hand whips out, snatching it to my chest.

Patient has left the building, Kai texts.

Not the words I was hoping for.

I look at my phone once more as I head up to bed that night. I set my alarm for four forty-five the next morning so I can meet the new Bitten Henry is sending to me, knowing full well the wake up won't be needed.

I won't be getting any sleep tonight.

chapter SIX

I T'S THE LONGEST NIGHT AND day ever. The only distraction comes from the woman who I meet down in the basement, Kai there to assist, but that only lasts a short amount of time. She didn't even try to bite me.

The day felt exceptionally long as I sat in the shop, too distracted to work on anything in the lab. Not many customers came in. Kai stayed at the shop all day, watching me, keeping one eye on the door the entire time, his headphones in and I just know he's blasting his island music.

I just kept staring at my phone, waiting for anyone to respond.

I'd texted Ian three more times. Called him twice. Called Alivia once. No answers. Finally, I dialed the landline at the House of Conrath. Nial picked up. But he had yet to hear anything either.

At five, Kai walks me home. He keeps trying to talk to me, to take my mind off of the possibility that my brother might be going to war against another House, but I just can't concentrate on anything else right now.

I pull my coat tighter around my body as we walk across the street. The temperatures have dipped. If the air shifts over the water just right, I'd wager we might have a chance of snow tonight.

"Do you want me to stay tonight?" Kai asks as my house comes into view.

"I don't think I'm going to be very good company tonight," I tell him as we cross the last street and start down my block.

"That's not the reason I'm asking," he says as he looks down at me. There's far too much weight in his eyes and it kills me.

I'm happy with the way our relationship is. But it's becoming more and more apparent, every day, that there's no going back for him. I can't lead him on.

"I'll be okay tonight," I say, stopping on the sidewalk right then and there. Kai takes two more steps before he realizes I've stopped in my tracks. He looks back at me in confusion.

"What?" he asks.

I bite my lower lip. A snake seems to have taken up residence in my stomach, coiling about, trying to slither up, choking the life out of me. I don't want to do what I have to do, but I can't just let it keep going on like this.

"Kai," I breathe out, twisting the hem of my coat awkwardly. "You can't keep letting helping me be the center of your life. You need to have your own life too, outside of walking me to and from work every day."

"What are you talking about?" he asks as his brows furrow. "If I don't protect you, who is going to?"

I shake my head. "It isn't just about protection. I appreciate everything you've done for me. It's so nice to know someone cares. But..." The words catch in my throat and I can't seem to get them out.

We've been friends for a long while now. But I can't be that girl who takes advantage of him.

Kai looks at me for a long time, understanding slowly growing in his eyes. And I see his features harden, little by little.

My blood turns cold and I'm so sorry.

But I can't keep giving him hope.

"But you don't feel about me the way I feel about you," he finally fills in the words.

I'm not an emotional person. It takes life and death to drag it out of me. But there's a sting at the back of my eyes.

"I do love you, Kai," I say. My voice sounds funny. Tight. Restricted. "You are my friend. My best friend. But I don't want to let you have hope that it's going to change into anything other than that for me."

"I'm not in any hurry, Elle," he says, his voice softening. "That could change someday."

I shake my head. "But I can't keep taking advantage of you. You do everything I ask, whenever I ask it. Helping me, I've let it consume you and take over your life. I have to let you go be you again. You need to find your identity outside of me. I think... I think it's time, Kai."

I know he knows exactly what I mean, because his expression grows from hurt, to disgusted. "You think I should take the cure? What, does that mean you're just done with me for good?"

I shake my head, throwing my hands up to stop him. "No! Not at all," I say, my voice pleading for him to understand. "It just means that I think we need to reset our relationship to something *normal*. If you're no longer a Bitten, I'm not just relying on you to keep the Bitten under control while I work. You can just be my friend. It can just be simple."

Kai shakes his head. "Nothing about my life has been simple in the last nine months. And…" he trails off. He shakes his head as his eyes drop from me to the sidewalk. "I don't know that I can take that big of a step back like this, Elle. I'm happy with the way we are now. And you just want to go and shred that all up and piece it back into something that looks entirely different."

My bottom lip quivers a touch. I swallow hard. "I think it's what's best."

His eyes finally rise back up to mine. He gives a little frustrated scoff and walks past me. Back in the direction of his house, away from mine.

"Please think about it," I call, turning to watch him go.

He makes no acknowledgement he heard me. Just walks down the road.

Away.

My giant friend, who loves music, and dancing, and has an amazing voice, but will never sing for others to hear. My friend who loves to cook and is always trying to fatten me up. My friend who has always been there at the drop of a hat.

He walks away. My chest aches as I see him go. But I can't be selfish.

Getting my legs to move isn't easy as I start back to my house. I'm stiff, frozen over.

I've never had a serious relationship in my life. The closest I've ever been to someone outside of my family is with Kai.

But when you love someone, you have to do what's best for them.

And I had to let him know the reality. That he needed to do what was best for him.

I take a shallow, shaky breath as I open the door and walk up the stairs to my apartment. Ready for a long, hot bath, I unlock my front door and step inside.

"You have no idea the amount of self-control that took to not step outside and intervene."

I jump about six inches in the air, dropping my keys as I close the door behind me. A tiny yelp escapes my lips, followed by a curse.

"Ian," I pant as my heart pounds in my chest. I swear again, bending to pick up my keys, as well as Shada, who stands beside my feet, hissing at my brother. And the man who sits beside him on the couch. "Lexington? What are you guys doing here?"

Lexington looks up at me, his vivid blue eyes nearly glowing in the dark room. I check to make sure the blinds are shut tightly and flip the light on. "I've been trying to get ahold of you all day."

"Yeah, I saw that," Ian says as he stands and shifts from one foot to the other, his arms crossed over his chest.

"You really should try to keep contact to a minimum for the next little while," Lexington pipes up, shifting forward, resting his forearms on his knees. "Charles' IT guy is kind of an idiot, but it wouldn't take too much skill to trace the calls to Ian's phone to your location."

I look over at my brother, looking for signs of injury. But he seems to be all in once piece.

"So, does that mean this feud isn't over?" I ask when he doesn't clarify. "Do I have anything to be worried about?"

Ian bites the inside of his lip and I can see the gears turning in his head. That means this is going to be complicated.

"It was a weird visit, we'll call it that," Lexington pipes up when my brother seems unable to form the words.

"What is that supposed to mean?" I ask, turning to Ian once more. "Spit it out."

Ian lets out a puff of a breath, weighed down and frustrated. "Charles is down to only five House members," he finally says. He sinks onto the arm of the couch. "When his House members were killed by Cora's army after Liv's coronation party, he escaped with only three other members. There were ten of them who didn't go to the party, that stayed in Vermont."

I never saw the aftermath of the slaughter, but the haunted look in Lexington's eyes right now tells me it must have been bad.

"After that day, the other House members got scared," Lexington fills in. "That's half the reason you join a House when you're a non-royal, there's strength in numbers. Half of their family had just been slaughtered."

There's a weight in his voice. Had Cyrus not forced the Allaways to trade some House members, Lexington would have left with them that night and likely been killed too.

"My guess is they saw Charles as weak after that," Ian carries on.

"And well, he's an idiot."

"And annoying as hell," Lexington interjects.

Ian nods in agreement. "I don't know how quick it all happened, but slowly, most of his House members left, either off on their own, or joining other Houses."

"I know at least five of them went to the House in Vegas," Lexington says. "I still had a few friends there. They've been gone for a year."

"But five House members are all that stayed?" I ask.

The number is shocking. Liv has been working on hers for seven years now, sitting at least at twenty-something members, and from what I know, she's a smaller House.

Ian nods. "He's been recruiting heavily for the past six months. Trying to bribe Born into swearing allegiance. Just last night he tried to buy off anyone from our House who wanted money more than a family."

"Did anyone bite?" I ask as my brows furrow.

Ian shakes his head. "They all know Charles' reputation."

"Some of us were loyal to him once," Lexington says, a dark look in his eyes. "Until we knew what better looked like."

"We told him to back off," Ian says. "Told him the threats need to stop. He agreed, but when you're outnumbered four to one, you'd better do what you're told."

I nod. Shada hisses and I set her down. She goes racing up the stairs. "So we're good then. You don't need to worry anymore."

Ian shakes his head. "I don't think this is over, Elle. Just as we were about to leave, Charles pulled me aside." Something clouds in Ian's face.

He's never been one that's very good at hiding his emotions. He wears everything on the surface. "He told me he knows it was our mother who killed his sister. This isn't just an Allaway against Conrath feud anymore, Elle. This is Allaway getting revenge against the Ward family."

A frozen stone drops in my stomach.

The mother who walked away from us so many years ago was a bad woman. Evil and twisted.

And even from the grave, she's bringing pain to our family.

"The Allaways are vengeful people," Lexington says in a low voice. "Charles and Chelsea were freaky close, even for being twins. He isn't just going to let this go."

I look from Lexington to Ian. The look he's giving me is a more intense version of the one he held every night as he locked me up in Lula's house.

"You think he's going to try and come after me for revenge," I clarify.

"Yes," Ian says.

A sister for a sister.

That reality sinks over the room like a choking fog. It presses on my chest, sinks into my bones.

"Did you kill him?" I ask.

My brother's eyes say he would have. "Killing a Royal is a guaranteed ticket back to *Roter Himmel*," he says. "And a painful execution. If I can't reason with him, I'll have to find another method of delivery."

Of death. That part is clear.

"I can't move you back home," Ian continues. "If he can come up with the bodies, he'll send spies. They'll expect me to hide you somewhere close to home where I can keep an eye on you."

"The Allaways are nuts, but they are a close family, other than murdering their mother when they came of age," Lexington says with a nod. "That's what they would do in this kind of situation. They'd never expect you to be hiding in their own territory."

"You're going to let me stay?" I say in awe as I look back at Ian.

The pained look in his eyes says he doesn't want to. "Lexington is right. The last place Charles is going to look is right under his own nose."

A smile begins forming on my lips, but the tortured look in my brother's eyes stops it from fully growing. "What?"

"This means that until I get this score settled we can't risk communication," he says. "They might trace phone calls. They could try to plant a bug in the House. They could have spies follow our people. We can't risk any form of regular communication."

"Regular," I repeat.

"Lexington can hide traces through the computer," Ian says, glancing over his shoulder at his fellow House member. "That will be the only way. It can't be often, we don't want to take any more risks than we have to. But he can facilitate."

"But you said you couldn't risk your people getting followed," I say in confusion. "Him traveling back and forth once a week is going to be noticed."

"He's staying," my brother says curtly. "And I mean in this house, in that bedroom across from yours."

"Excuse me?" I raise an eyebrow, my mouth not fully closing.

Ian stands, walking over to me, resting his hands on my shoulders. "I know you've got that Bitten," he says through the annoyance in his voice. Little does he understand the mess I've just made. "But even you know Born are stronger than Bitten. And Lexington knows how Charles thinks. He knows the Allaway habits and ways of ruling. You need someone like him here, Elle."

I look away from my brother to the man sitting on the couch. The look in his eyes tells me he's a little conflicted about this situation. But he's proven his loyalty to the House of Conrath over the past six years. He's not going to fail Alivia now.

"And Liv approved this plan?" I say quietly.

Ian nods. "It was one hundred percent her idea."

I bite my lower lip. I don't have a choice in this matter, and I know it.

And truthfully, I probably should have someone, because I'm pretty sure I screwed things up beyond repair with Kai.

"Okay," I breathe. I give a little nod, feeling the fight seep out of my body. "We'll make this work."

Something lightens in Ian's expression. He expected me to fight this more. Expected the argument I usually give him over stuff like this. But he doesn't know the fully story of the past hour.

"Okay," he breathes, allowing a tiny smile. He pulls me into his arms, hugging me tight. "I promise, I'll get this situation taken care of. I'll do whatever I have to."

"I know you will." I squeeze him tight, grateful to have him here with me once more. And I don't know how long it will be until I will see him again.

"I need to go," he says into my hair. "The longer I stay the more at risk I'm putting you. We'll talk in a few days, okay?"

I nod as he lets me go and takes a step away. That's when I notice the bags beside the fireplace, next to Lexington.

I really had no choice about him staying.

"You let anything happen to my sister and I'll be wearing your balls for a necklace, you know that, right?" Ian says as he takes a step for the door. The look in his eyes says he's dead serious.

"I think everyone knows that when it comes to your family, you're always do or die," Lexington says, holding his hands up in surrender. "I'll keep her safe. Promise."

My brother fixes him with a deathly gaze, no joking around. He turns back to me as he opens the door. I follow him, holding it open.

"Don't…take any unnecessary risks, please," he begs. "Not until we get this resolved."

I smile at him, but don't say a word. He knows I can't really promise that, not in this world we were born into. "Travel safe," I offer instead.

Ian presses a kiss to the top of my head, and with a pained smile, he takes off.

Slowly, I close the door, locking it when it's shut. And turn to my new housemate.

"So," Lexington says awkwardly as he stands. He claps his hands together, seemingly unsure of where to look. "It's been a while."

"Yeah," I respond, just as awkward.

"Like, what? Three years since we've seen each other?" he says, giving me this squinty-eyed look as he tries to figure it out.

"Four and a half," I say with a little smile.

Wow. I haven't been back to Silent Bend since I left for college.

"Four and a half," he says with a nod. "You've…you've grown up a lot since then."

I give a little chuckle and shake my head as I walk out of the living room and into the kitchen.

Living in Liv's House for two years meant I got to know some of the occupant vampires pretty well. Cameron, Liv's best friend, was always friendly and down for inviting everyone to everything. Nial was like a loving uncle. Leigh took it upon herself to make me her pedicure buddy. May tried looking after me like I was her own granddaughter.

But some of the other House members I tried to avoid, or just had very little contact with. Markov, who once tried to drink from me. Danny, who was just plain terrifying looking. Trinity, who hated everyone.

Lexington and I had always been hardly aware that the other existed.

But I'm sure going to get to know him better now. Whether I want to or not.

chapter
SEVEN

"**A**FTER YOU," LEXINGTON SAYS WITH a smile, stepping aside and letting me down the stairs first. I awkwardly give him a thin-lipped one as I step around him and walk down the stairs, immediately hooking into the kitchen to grab some breakfast quickly before heading to work.

After Ian left last night, Lexington pretty much spent the night unpacking his things in the guest bedroom and wandering the house and the rooftop, looking for weak spots. We said maybe ten words to each other for the rest of the night.

I sort of awkwardly hid in my room with the door cracked in case he needed anything. I didn't know what to say or how to suddenly occupy my own house with another person living in it.

I quickly dart up to the garden, gathering a few plants before heading back inside. Lexington leans against the kitchen counter, biting into an apple, waiting for me.

"It seems like I remember hearing something about you having, like, a poison garden back in Silent Bend," he says as he follows me out front and waits while I lock the door. "Was that true or am I mixing things up?"

"It was true," I say as I quickly set off down the sidewalk.

"I swear, I remember you being a kid when you lived back in Silent Bend," he says with a chuckle. "Like, weren't you this big?" He holds his hand up to chest height. "What's a kid doing with a dangerous garden like that?"

I fix him with a deadly stare as we walk swiftly, side by side. "I was almost seventeen when you moved into the House."

Lexington laughs, shrugging his shoulders. "My bad. Guess I wasn't paying that close attention."

I shake my head and continue walking as fast as I can.

Lexington and I never talked and all the memories I have of him are sarcastic and stirring the pot. Nial and Danny were constantly annoyed with him. He has a very loud mouth but didn't have much of a filter. Apparently that hasn't changed much in the past four years.

"But seriously, you still like working with plants I guess?" he says as we cross the street, darting through the busy Boston morning traffic, to shortcut through the Boston Public Garden.

"I have a degree in botany, so yeah, I guess you could say I still like working with plants." I dart around a crowd of people standing in the middle of the sidewalk. Lexington drops behind me, weaving in and out of people.

"I'm guessing Ian already told you, but just to reiterate: don't ever call me by my real name when we're out in public," I say as we head to the shop. "To everyone in Boston, I'm Penny Jones."

"Got it," he says simply.

The morning dawns over the horizon, shooting between the buildings, making its way to the early risers on their way to work. I look to the side, marveling at how Lexington, a Born vampire with permanently dilated eyes is able to walk through the morning without being in agonizing pain.

Henry's ingenuity is something I'm greatly jealous of.

"What?" Lexington suddenly asks, catching me staring.

I shake my head and look back in the direction I'm walking.

Oleander Apothecary waits for me just down the road like a loving friend. Just the sight of my shop brings an intense amount of comfort to me. I unlock the door, inhaling deep as I step inside.

"Whoa," Lexington says, taking everything in with awe as he follows me inside. "I kind of feel like I'm back in 1868. I once visited a shop that looked just like this for a bad case of what is now known as the chicken pox."

"When were you born?" I ask, because suddenly that's the kind of thing I should know about my new housemate.

"1851," he says, looking around while I hang my things up. He stares at a line of roll-ons for headaches. "Just north of here, actually. In Maine, right on the border."

"And you Resurrected at what? Twenty-three?" I guess as I look through my schedule. I have six customers coming in to pick up custom orders today.

"Close, twenty-four," he says with a smile as he moves to another shelf. I roll my eyes as he studies the Adore Me perfume, knowing what's coming. "Do people really think that all this stuff works?"

I kind of want to punch him right now. "All of this stuff *does* work," I say as I pull two of the orders out from the cabinet below the counter. "Except that stuff, sort of. Unfortunately it's what sells best."

He grabs a bottle of it from off the shelf and sprays five squirts into the air.

"No!" I yell, but it's too late. He's stuck his face right in the middle of the plume and takes a deep inhale. I sigh, leaning back.

Lexington scrunches up his nose, a very dramatic look on his face, and a moment later, sneezes, three times. Very loudly.

"Uh," he says, squeezing the bridge of his nose as he blinks fast, looking away from the light. "That's one potent perfume you made there."

He blinks several more times, temporarily blinded from the sneezing fit. With watery eyes, he looks back up at me.

And keeps staring at me for a moment that lasts too long. "You really have grown up a lot in the last four and a half years."

"Oh, please no," I say as my shoulders sag. I shake my head.

"What?" he asks as a dopy smile forms on his lips and he takes slow, deliberate swagger steps toward me. "You know you really have blossomed into something—"

"You realize what's happening right now, right?" I say, crossing my arms over my chest and giving him a look.

"What?" he asks with a laugh. I just continue to fix him with a hard stare. He blinks twice, but I see the gears start turning in his head and suddenly understanding dawns in his eyes. He looks over at the bottle of perfume in his hand. "Oh. Oh no."

"Yeah," I say. "You just went and inhaled the love perfume that does have a little scientific backing to it."

"Oh no," he says, keeping his lips puckered. "I just... And you're there. And we..."

"Don't worry," I say with a sigh as I turn to head into the lab. "It's extremely short lived. You'll be fine by supper time."

"And what am I supposed to do in the meantime?" he calls. His footsteps suddenly shuffle and he hurries to follow after me.

I bend over, grabbing the third custom order from the fridge under the counter. I find it and straighten, setting it on the counter.

I turn to see Lexington, staring exactly where he shouldn't be looking.

"Just try to keep your eyes off of my ass until then," I say in annoyance.

"Right," he says, his eyes snapping up to mine.

"DON'T FORGET, ONE DOSE AFTER breakfast, another just before you go to bed." I put Aneska Cortan's custom made inhalant into a bag, along with the relaxation cream she buys now and then.

"Thank you, Penny," she says, her Croatian accent thick. "You get a replacement? I'll admit, the last one was nice to look at, but this one..."

She trails off suggestively as she eyes Lexington up and down.

He gives a little laugh, clearly flattered at the woman's words. "Well, thank you, I think."

She winks at him, taking her bag and heading to the door.

"You do get some weirdos in here," Lexington says from his perch on my stool in the corner. "But I think the clientele is growing on me."

"Don't flirt with my customers," I say, resisting an eye roll as I head back into the lab. Lexington, of course, follows me.

"Never," he says suggestively. I look over my shoulder to see his eyes rolling up and down me again.

"Stop it," I snap at him. Even if a little smile pulls on my lips when I turn back to the worktable. I don't often get to see my products work right in front of my eyes. The clients take them and go, to use them at home. I've always been most self-conscious about my love perfume. It's nice to see it does kind of work in some form.

I should have called it lust spray.

"I swear I'm trying," he says, but I can still feel his eyes on me.

I sigh. Just a few more hours and it will wear off.

I turn to the burner and light it. Setting a pot on top, I pour some water into it.

A row of spices and ingredients line the shelf above me and my eyes run down the line until I come to the chili peppers. I grab the jar, and next the pepper.

"What are you making?" Lexington asks, coming up to stand beside me.

"Attacker spray," I say. I find my stone and pestle. "Here, you might as well be useful." I set them in front of him and put seven dried peppers into the well. "Grind these up."

"Is this pepper spray?" he asks as he awkwardly begins crushing the peppers.

"Pepper spray would be it's more mild, timid cousin," I say, smiling as I set to gathering the other ingredients.

"You thought there was a need for something more aggressive than pepper spray?" he asks, and to my surprise, something softens in his voice.

I swallow hard, recalling the night, my first year at Northwestern. My scream. His roar of anger. The gripping hands that left so many bruises.

"Elle." A soft voice pulls me back into the room. I feel Lexington walk up behind me, the heat of his body warming my own. "What happened?"

"Don't worry about it," I say, putting more effort into the task at hand. "It was a long time ago."

"Elle," he says, his tone firm but caring. "I'm not here to judge you. I just...I'm here to listen if you want."

I look over my shoulder at him, and am shocked at the sincerity in his voice. I study him for a moment, trying to decide if he's being serious.

But the intensity in his eyes pulls open the tight lid I keep on my emotions.

Something in my chest aches.

Wants to get out.

I bite my lower lip, putting more force into the way I cut the barbed part off of the stinging nettle. "I was a freshman," I say, even though I don't know why I'm letting the words fall from my lips. "It was late. I was walking back to my dorm from the library. I'd heard there was a sicko out there, doing things to girls he shouldn't be doing. So I bought some pepper spray."

The scissors slip in my hand and suddenly a flash of pain sears into my index finger. I hiss in pain.

"Whoa," Lexington calls, pulling my hands away from the very painful plant I'm working with. The one that's now worked it's way into a bleeding wound. "Is this what I think it is?"

"Yeah," I hiss through the pain as tears well into my eyes. Stinging nettle direct into an open wound blurs my vision with pain. "Go grab one of the bottles labeled *Sooth Me*."

He disappears for all of two seconds before he suddenly reappears in front of me, the container in hand. He sets to wiping the blood and applying the cream.

"This creep found you, didn't he?" Lexington asks as he takes care of my injured finger.

I nod as I watch him. "I was prepared. I had the pepper spray in hand, so when he grabbed me from behind, all I had to do was turn, point, and spray."

"What happened?" he asks, finished applying the ointment. I point for the first aid kit affixed to the wall. He grabs it and digs through for some gauze.

"It just pissed him off," I say as my voice grows quieter. "I've never heard a human make a sound like that. Like … like an animal. He grabbed me around the throat and shoved me down on the ground."

Lexington swears as he wraps my finger. His grip tightens marginally in anger.

"I fought back, so he hit me," I say. "I sprayed him again. His face sure turned red, his eyes were watering like crazy. But it wasn't enough to disable him."

"Elle," Lexington breathes. He takes my hand into his, holding it gently. The look he gives me is one you'd use with a broken and wounded bird.

"He didn't rape me." I stop everything. I swallow past the hard rock in my throat. "A group of guys came along just then and heard me scream. They pulled him off of me, beat the crap out of him, and called the cops."

"So he got put away?" Lexington asks. My eyes finally meet his, and I see the anger and the pity and sadness in his.

"Yeah," I say, my voice coming out strained. "He'll spend the next forty years in prison."

"Elle," Lexington says in a whisper. "That's awful."

"I was the lucky one," I say with the nod of my head. "The other six girls weren't."

I pull my hand away from his and turn back to the peppers that are only half crushed. I dump them into the boiling water anyway. "I'd never made anything intended to use on humans before then," I continue as I stir them in. "Everything had been to use against vampires up until that point. But I went to the chemistry lab that next day and started the recipe for this. No one will keep walking after being sprayed with this."

Lexington swears once more.

The bell above the door in the shop dings, and I look up in panic.

I'm not ready to just turn past trauma off like that and go help someone.

"I got this," Lexington says, holding a hand up, as if to push my panic back. "I'll let you know if they need you."

"Thank you," I say, truly meaning it.

I listen to the conversation as this newcomer shops for a gift for his girlfriend.

And I wonder if just maybe I inhaled a little bit of that love perfume, too.

I've never told anyone the story of the assault. Not Ian. Not Alivia. Certainly not Kai.

I don't tell anyone anything.

Yes, I've known who Lexington is for the past six years, but before yesterday we've probably only said two-dozen words to one another.

I didn't expect to actually have a meaningful conversation with him.

I'm just wrapping the spray up, setting it aside to cool, when he walks back into the lab.

"Everything go okay?" I ask.

He nods. "You weren't kidding about that love perfume being your bestseller. The guy bought three bottles." He gives a little smile. "Your register is pretty basic. Wasn't too hard to figure out how to ring him up."

I nod, holding his gaze. "Thank you. I didn't mean…I didn't mean to go into something so deep."

"It's okay," he says, shaking his head. And I see it in his eyes. He really means it. "I'm glad you did."

I offer him a little smile, hoping it looks genuine.

"Need any more help?" he asks.

"So, you just let them sleep it off here in the basement?"

Lexington looks down at the woman sleeping on the cot. I stand in the corner of the room, arms folded over my chest.

"Yeah," I say, talking quiet, even though I know I won't wake her. She has about nine more hours until she will wake up.

"Incredible," he says with a little smile on his lips. His hands are pushed into his pockets, his shoulders relaxed. There's something easy and casual about his stance.

I wonder what that's like.

"I'm ready to go," I say, nodding my head toward the door.

Lexington takes one last look around the clinic, a look of awed disbelief in his eyes. But he follows me out, and I lock up.

"Not gonna' lie, these tunnels are a little creepy," he says as we walk down the hall and to the stairs.

"There's a lot of history in Boston," I say. "Not all of it is visible from the surface."

"You know, I lived my entire life within a few hours of Boston, but until yesterday, I'd never actually visited the city." He follows me as I grab my things and we walk out the door of the shop, locking it behind us. "You're closed on Saturdays, right?"

I made an affirmative noise.

"So how about you show me around the city," he says, hands still in his pockets, walking slow and easy. "Be my tour guide?"

I look over at him, really looking. "I think the love spray hasn't worn off just yet."

"I swear, I feel much better now," he says with a laugh. "But come on. I mean, we're stuck with each other for the indefinite future. Might as well make the best of it, right?"

I look over at him. The expression on his face is so hopeful. Excited. So…happy.

"You know, you're different than I remember you."

"What's that supposed to mean?" he asks, giving me another one of his looks that I can't really describe. He has a lot of them. Lexington has a very expressive face.

I shrug. "I guess you just sort of came off as this sarcastic jerk when I first met you. You were always making these snide comments and trying to piss everyone off."

He chuckles and looks forward. "Well, you know, I had just been given up by the family I'd been a part of for over thirty years. I think just about anyone would have been a little bitter."

"I'll give you that," I say with a nod. My stomach suddenly growls, the evening stretching on late.

"Someone really needs to start taking a lunch break," he says, raising an eyebrow at me. "Look there. There's a pizzeria right down the block. Let the tour of Boston begin!"

And like it's no big deal whatsoever, Lexington grabs my hand, and takes off at a jog the rest of the way down the block. "Holy ice fingers, woman!" he laughs at my ever frozen hands.

I chuckle, struggling to keep up with him as we slow in front of the pizzeria.

"I will survive until we make it home," I say, my face flushing in embarrassment as we run through the front doors. The hostess gives us a surprised look, which quickly changes over to annoyance.

"Why wait?" he winks at me, telling the woman that it's just the two of us.

She grabs two menus and leads us through a maze of tables. Seating us, she walks away.

"What's good here?" Lexington asks, his eyes grazing down the menu.

"I've actually never been here before," I confess as I look through their many, many options.

"You're kidding, right?" he asks with a laugh. "It's a block from your shop. I've heard rumors about Boston's pizza. And you've never stepped foot inside?"

A little smile pulls in the corners of my mouth. "I don't really go out," I explain. "Like ever. I go home and order delivery. I mean, it's usually just me. I've always been a little lame, but not lame enough to go out to eat at a restaurant by myself."

"No one would ever call someone as badass as you, lame," Lexington says, shaking his head as he continues to read down the menu.

His words draw a little smile on my face, which I hide behind my own menu.

chapter
EIGHT

S ATURDAY BRINGS A DIP IN temperature. The mid-November
air has a bite to it, alluding to the bitter winter that is coming. It's
the only time of year that I'm tempted to return to the South. I
have yet to acclimate to actual winters. Besides the curse storm year,
Silent Bend has always had such mild winters.

"I didn't realize how much I liked the South until last winter when
the House spent Thanksgiving dinner out on the lawn by the river,"
Lexington says as we make our way through the Public Garden and into
Boston Common. "It was seventy-one degrees. I was wearing shorts."

I chuckle, comparing the stark differences. I'm wearing boots and
a wool coat, a scarf around my neck, gloves, and a knitted band around
my head to cover my ears. Lexington is dressed similarly.

"I'll admit, it's still something I'm getting used to. The cold," I clarify.

We cut through the park, past the bandstand and aim for the beginning of the Freedom Trail. There aren't as many tourists out this time of year, it's getting a little too cold for that, but there are still plenty of bodies about.

"Do people ever question you about your accent?" Lexington asks, looking over at me.

I shrug. "Like I said, I don't go out much. At least half of my customers at the Apothecary are regulars, so they're used to it. But some people ask."

"You certainly sound and look like the incarnation of a Southern Belle," he says, smiling as we walk along.

I turn my face away from him, hiding my smile.

It's something I tried to hide the entire time I was at Northwestern. My accent is strong, having grown up in a tiny town in Mississippi. To me it was normal. Everyone from back home sounded just like me. But in Illinois, it stuck out like a sore thumb. Brought a lot of attention, and that's something I've never wanted.

But here in Boston, in a mix of a lot of different accents, I finally accepted that I just needed to be me, and that was okay.

"In case you're suddenly embarrassed," Lexington observes. I look over to see him studying me. "It's incredibly adorable. And I swear that's coming from me, not that stuff I inhaled two days ago."

I know I'm blushing, but his expression is so genuine, I don't hide my face again.

When he looks away, checking out the landmarks around us, I take the time to really study him.

He's probably around six feet tall, just a little shorter than Ian. His shoulders are broad and his body well defined without being the gym rat type. Dirty blond hair sits atop his head, always somewhere between messy styled and bed head. It's hard to tell if he actually puts the effort into it or if he just rolls out of bed that way.

Somehow it really suits his personality.

His eyes are bright blue; they're beautiful, really. And it's incredible that as a vampire, he's able to walk around during the day with no pain— thanks to implants in his eyes that Henry created. Artificial pupils that dilate and filter out painful UV rays.

His lips are thin, framed by a beard that I get the feeling that is there more out of laziness than purposeful style. I know I've seen him clean shaven before.

Lexington's appearance could be described as semi-purposefully permanently disheveled.

Casual and relaxed, always without too much thought. But it all blends into something that works, and entirely captures his personality.

"You're staring."

I jump slightly, instantly pulling my eyes away from him. And feel my face flush hard.

"It's okay," he says without looking at me as we continue walking down the trail. "It's not fair really. I have an unfair advantage, being a vampire, I can just sense some things, you know? See, you're a human, and while you're certainly one of the more deadly, cool ones I know, you don't have all these extra senses. So you have no idea when I'm staring."

I bite my lower lip, fighting the smile. I look away from him, because I can't stand the idea of him seeing it. "So are you saying that's something you've been doing frequently?"

"Maybe," he says so casually.

It's really not fair how easily he keeps his cool.

"Hey, let's go check this place out," he says, tilting his head toward the Park Street Church. His eyes meet mine, and I see it all there. He's giving me a way out of this awkward conversation without embarrassing me.

I give him a small smile as a thank you, and follow him across the street.

"You know, I was raised as a Lutheran," he says as we wait behind a few people to enter the church.

"Oh yeah?" I say. The group of women in front of us in line chat loudly, too loud considering we're about to enter a church. One of them does a little double glance over her shoulder, her eyes locking on Lexington.

"Yep," he says, oblivious to her approving stare. Except he's a vampire, and I'm sure he's not really unaware. "My mother was devout. Took us every week. Made sure we read our scriptures every night. Martin Luther was an ancestor of mine, and she was extremely proud of that fact."

We step inside behind the group. The church is rather simple, really, compared to some of the others in Boston. Rows of pews. Simple chandeliers. A grand piano. A cross at the front of the room.

"Did you believe the same as she did?" I ask as we slowly make a loop through the chapel. I've read all the historical signs before. Lexington's eyes briefly graze over them and I'm sure he can read them much faster than I can.

Lexington shrugs. "I guess. I never really doubted my mother and she believed it all so deeply. I just sort of took it at face value. I didn't have anything against it, so I kept going."

It really doesn't take long to complete our loop. Within a few minutes, we make our way back down the front steps and head back onto the trail.

"I guess it just got hard to attach to religion though when I Resurrected," he says as he stuffs his hands in his pockets and we continue down the trail.

"Did you know?" I ask.

It's a question that defines so much of a vampire's life, the line between a choice and an accident. Fear and certainty.

Lexington nods. "My mother didn't know at first though. She married my father and I was a year old before she caught him feeding on one of the maids." He looks over at me, probably expecting to find an expression of shock on my face, but I've seen way too much to be surprised by something that simple. "She couldn't cope though. Knowing what he was, being the religious woman she was. She couldn't accept it all. I think my father must have really loved her, because he finally let her go. Let her divorce him. Not sure how to feel about the fact that he walked away from me so easily though."

"You never saw him again?" I ask.

He shakes his head. "My mother would write him letters now and then, telling him about me. But he left when I was three and I never saw him again. I tried to find him once, about a hundred years ago, but I think he must have been dead. No trace of him."

"I'm sorry," I offer. "I imagine that must have been hard."

Lexington shrugs his shoulders. "You know that saying, 'time heals all wounds?' It's true for the most part. I've had a long time to get over it."

He said the other day that he was born in 1851. He's had over 150 years to get over it.

Immortality is the part of vampirism that I have the hardest time wrapping my head around.

I'll die in seventy or so years. But so many of the others that I know will still look the same as they do now, living on for eternity so long as they can avoid a stake to the heart or a beheading.

"But she didn't hide what you were from you?" I ask, returning to the history of Lexington.

He shakes his head. "No, she made sure I knew what my history was. Took me a long time to fully understand what that meant. I don't think it really connected until I was probably about sixteen or so, when she tried to explain to me that I had a choice in when I wanted to stop aging."

"I can't even imagine," I say. Because to stop aging, he had to die first.

"Yeah," he says with a short laugh. "The concept of dying, but not staying dead was a little hard to get a good grasp on. She'd been telling me that someday I'd want to drink blood, but the death part was a little out there for me."

I've grown so desensitized to everything in the vampire world, but origin stories from the mouths of those who have lived it put things in perspective.

"My younger siblings stood guard around the house when I decided twenty-four sounded just right to stop aging."

I look around to be sure no one is too close to overhear the very peculiar story I'm being told. Thankfully no one walks nearby.

"Half siblings?" I ask.

He nods. "My mom remarried when I was six. Had three more kids."

I look over at him, my brows furrowing. "You know, I've known you for six years, yet I just realized I have no idea what your last name is."

He laughs, shaking his head. "Lexington Dawes. It's nice to meet you, Elle Ward."

"Be nice," I say, giving him a little look.

He laughs again. "Laugh a little. It's healthy for you."

I just shake my head. I've smiled and laughed more in the last three days than I did in the previous three months.

"So what's the deal with the strange name?" I ask. "Can't say I've ever met, or even heard of another Lexington."

"I came first, dubbed by my mother as Lexington," he explains. "Next followed my sister, Concord. Then my brother Lincoln, and lastly my baby sister Cambridge."

"Aw," I say, dawning lighting in my mind. "The Battle of Lexington and Concord."

"And all the surrounding battles and history," he says, nodding. "My great-grandfather was a big to do with it all. So my mother honored him by naming us after our legacy."

"So you really do have some deep roots in Massachusetts."

He nods. "Our family moved north to Maine in the early eighteen hundreds, but my family history is spread all throughout the New England area."

I look over at him as we walk. "I get why it was so hard for you when the Allaways essentially exiled you to the South."

He looks over at me, his expression deep and grateful. "Roots run deep. And living your very long life for so long in one place makes it hard to uproot and transplant."

I nod. "But you've been happy being a part of the House of Conrath, right?"

"Yeah," he says as a smile pulls at his mouth. "I mean, I was a part of the House of Allaway for thirty-two years. After slowly losing all of my siblings to old age and disease over the years, and being on my own for a long time, I started getting lonely. A brief infatuation with a woman who was one of their House members brought me to them, and I never left."

A small cemetery spreads out to the side of King's Chapel. Old and ancient, the headstones are well worn, some of them difficult to read after hundreds of years of weathering. We slowly wander through, taking in the names of the dead.

"I had some friendships in the House of Allaway," Lexington says quietly. "But it wasn't family. I can't say there was any real love in that House. After the trade, once I finally got over myself, I started seeing that Alivia actually cared about all of us. It had been a long time since I'd been a part of a family, but I still remembered what that felt like. She might have had a rocky start, but Alivia is a good person."

I nod. My sister-in-law had a long road in figuring out her place as a Royal and a House leader, but once she got there, she shined. And continues to do so.

"I'm sorry you're out of place once more," I say, looking over at him.

"I'm sure it isn't easy being sent away from your home again."

He reaches out and takes my hand, giving it a little squeeze. "I can't say I mind. As much as I do enjoy being part of the House of Conrath, it's kind of nice being back close to home."

I give him a little smile, tucking a loose hair behind my ear.

"And are your fingers always colder than icicles?" he laughs.

"And somehow my toes are always worse," I chuckle back.

chapter NINE

THERE ARE A LOT OF historical sites to see along the Freedom Trail. The Boston Massacre Site, Faneuil Hall, the Paul Revere House. America is young compared to a lot of countries, but Boston's history is several hundred years deep, and its foundation is solid.

Twilight falls on the city as we round into the Paul Revere Mall, which is more of a park than anything. The end of our trip today is in sight, the Old North Church, when Lexington suddenly stiffens, stopping dead in his tracks.

"What is it?" I ask. Every muscle in my body instinctually tightens. My hand slips into my purse where my dart gun rests.

"Follow me," he says quietly. His hand wraps around mine, and he's suddenly pulling me off the trail and back behind a building. The second we're out of sight, he loops my hand over his head and his hands grip me, hoisting me up on his back.

And then we're flying.

Vampires are incredibly fast. So fast the human eye can make out little more than a blur.

That's what the buildings, people, and cars around us look like to me.

Lexington darts through the city, running so fast I can't even feel his feet beating against the sidewalks and roads. So fast the scream catches in my throat.

He suddenly comes to a halt and my stomach heaves. My head spins and I nearly fall over when he puts me down.

A noise settles into my ears, one I've heard before.

A blissful moan accompanied by a sucking sound.

"Stay here," Lexington says quietly, his eyes fixed on an alleyway. My line of sight follows him as he darts across the road.

There, in the alleyway, stands a woman, completely motionless, while a man and a woman latch onto her neck, drinking.

"Hey guys," Lexington says, walking up. They startle, dropping the woman, who collapses to the ground. "How's your evening going?"

"We're not sharing," the man laughs, his eyes glowing brilliant red in the darkening night. "So if a threesome is what you're looking for, you might wanna' check elsewhere."

"Not tonight," Lexington says, trying very hard to keep his tone casual. "But you know, both of you drinking from the same person is a pretty quick way to kill someone or turn them."

The woman laughs. "So. We've been drinking as much as we like and there's been no repercussions for having fun. Not in years. There's no one left to say no."

She drops to the ground and her fangs extend. Lexington darts forward, dragging the unconscious woman away from the vampire. "Maybe not," he says, backing away another two steps when she hisses at him. "But see, there's this new thing from King Cyrus, that if you turn anyone, it's punishable by death."

"Not if no one is around to narc," the man snarls, taking a step toward Lexington.

"Really guys," he says, his tone tired and impatient. "You really want to make this get ugly?"

"You're the one who came at us," the woman says. "We were minding our own business."

Suddenly she lunges forward, her hands outstretched. With one hand, Lexington wraps his fingers around her throat, spinning and flinging her against the side of the building.

I jump forward a step, pulling my dart gun from my bag. My heart pounds in my chest.

The man jumps, sailing through the air.

The shot is perfect.

I press the narrow shaft to my lips.

And blow.

The dart hits him in the neck, just as he drops on top of Lexington.

His entire body instantly starts seizing up. He rolls off of Lexington, his muscles twitching, hissing in pain as he curls into a ball on the sidewalk.

The woman, seeing her partner incapacitated, roars in anger and rushes at Lexington as he sets the drained woman on the ground. Her hands wrap around his throat as I load another dart into my gun.

He slams her back against the building, his jaw clenched tight, his face coiled into a snarl. His eyes instantly flash from blue to brilliant, shining red. Black veins sprout out from his eyes, racing over his face.

A noise down the road pulls my eyes to the left. A group of young men laugh and talk as they walk down the sidewalk.

Straight toward us.

"Lexington," I breathe, knowing he'll hear me.

He glances in my direction, but it's enough distraction for the woman to push away from the wall, sending them crashing to the other side of the alley. Lexington's head bounces off the brick wall.

The group continues down the road, oblivious to the scene they're about to witness.

"Lexington," I say, urgency bleeding into my voice.

With a grunt, he spins away from the wall, grabbing her by the front of her shirt. He whips her through the air, slamming her down on the ground onto her back. In the same movement, he pulls a stake from the inside pocket of his jacket, and slams it down into her chest.

He stands, huffing hard, and straightens his clothes. He takes one step out of the alley, checking on the position of the oncoming group before darting back into the alley. In a blur, he disappears down the alley, dragging the two Born. When he reappears, he crooks a finger at me.

I run across the street, catching the eyes of the group, but disappear into the alley with Lexington.

He scoops the woman up into his arms, and we set out quickly down the alley.

"Is she still alive?" I ask as I struggle to keep up with his quick pace.

"Barely," he says, looking down at her as the glow in his eyes fades. "She's lost a lot of blood. You got any of that cure with you?"

"Of course," I say, reaching into my bag. I keep three doses on me at all times, plus the one around my neck for myself if ever needed.

"Give it to her now," he says as we tuck around the corner of the alley. I glance back just in time to see the group come into view of the alley. I catch the eye of one of the guys, just before slipping around the corner.

I take out a needle and jab it into her shoulder, pressing the plunger.

"We need to take her to a hospital," I say. "She won't turn, but without turning, she might die. She'll need a big transfusion."

Lexington nods, and I pull up the closest hospital on my phone.

"See that coffee shop?" he says as we get to the end of this alley. He nods his head in the direction of it, across the street and down the block a little way. "I want you to wait for me there. I'm going to get her to the hospital, she needs to get there quick. You got more of those toxins?"

I nod. "I'm okay. You get her to help."

He meets my eyes, looking for confirmation that I'm good. He nods once he finds it, and instantly, he's gone.

I wait anxiously with a chai tea between my hands for twenty minutes at the coffee shop. My right leg bounces up and down, anxiety crawling through my veins.

I've been in this city for two years now. And this is the first time I've ever had a run in with any Born.

Born being reckless. Feeding on someone out in the open. Not unnerved by the possibility of being caught.

This is so wrong.

Darkness fully blankets the city when at 7:23 Lexington finally pulls the door open and steps inside.

Relief washes through my system as his eyes search the shop for me. I'm on my feet, walking toward him and his eyes finally find me.

"She going to be okay?" I ask quietly as we step back outside. He walks fast, heading generally back in the direction of my house, which is miles from here.

"I think so," he says, keeping his voice down. His eyes dart all over the place. His shoulders are tight, his knees slightly bent. He's on edge, ready to fight again. "I dropped her off right in front of the emergency room doors when no one was looking. I waited to make sure someone found her. They took her in. Her heart was still beating, so I think she's in the clear."

I nod. "Good." My mind is reeling, going through all the implications of what this means. "You took care of those Born?"

He nods. "Yeah, they won't be causing any more trouble any time soon."

That's for sure. At least one of them is dead.

"Lexington," I breathe as we continue down the road at a fast pace. "I've never heard of a Born attacking at random in the city. They weren't even hiding."

"Word must be spreading that the House of Allaway has shrunk," he says. A homeless man steps forward, rambling and reaching a hand out toward us. Lexington takes my hand in his and pulls us to the other side of the road, picking up his pace. I can barely keep up and he doesn't let go of my hand. "The vampires in this region must be realizing they can get away with this kind of shit and that no one is going to come after them."

"This is bad," I breathe. "The Houses are the only things that keep this secret in check. If there's no governing, no fear of reprimand from the local regents or word getting to the King…"

"This could get out of hand real fast," Lexington finishes for me.

chapter
TEN

THE SCREEN'S GLOW ILLUMINATES LEXINGTON'S face as
he taps away at his laptop. I arrange the pages we've printed
on my dining table, taping the last few together. In all, the
fourteen pages create one giant map of the New England area.

The general area of the Allaway rule.

"Got another one in Michigan," Lexington says as he shakes his
head. He tells me the town and I mark it with a red pen on the map.

"That puts us up to seventeen blatant attacks in the last six months,"
I breathe. My eyes dart all over the map. The attacks are concentrated
most central to Vermont, the heart of the Allaway rule, thinning out
toward their borders.

Ten attacks in New York alone. Three in Pennsylvania. And one
each in Maine, Massachusetts, Ohio and Virginia.

"That's all I'm seeing in the past six months that are obvious,"

Lexington says as he tips back in his chair on two legs. He laces his fingers behind his head, still staring at the screen. "Comparing it to the other three quarters of the States and their House rule, this is getting to be a problem. There's been one attack under Conrath rule, and that was pretty nuts." He shakes his head knowingly. "And there's been three out West. Compared to *seventeen* in this area."

"It kind of sounds like Charles has just given up," I say as I affix tape to the back of our makeshift map. I hang it on the wall directly across from the table. Too many red marks, each of them representing a report of a death where the victim had fang marks in their neck. We haven't even touched missing persons reports. It would be impossible to tell which of those were due to a vampire turning them, or dying and their bodies just never being found.

"This is going to be noticed by Cyrus," Lexington says, sliding the laptop aside. He leans forward, his elbows on the table, cupping his chin in his hands as his eyes study the map.

"People die when the King comes around," I observe. The fear that preceded his arrival in Silent Bend was a tangible, choking thing.

Lexington nods. "Someone's here."

A knock sounds on the door and a second later, it swings open.

Instantly, Lexington disappears and there's a yell from the door and a thud as something hard hits the wall. I turn to see Kai pressed up against the wall beside the door, his eyes glowing brilliant yellow. Lexington has his hand around Kai's throat, his fingers digging deep into his skin, a stake pressed sharply into the base of his rib cage.

"Stop!" I yell, clambering from my chair, darting to their side. I claw at Lexington's hands. "Kai is a friend."

Lexington's eyes dart to mine, searching for confirmation. They glow brilliant red. "A friend who just walks in in the middle of the night?"

The clock above the couch reads 1:28. I hadn't realized how much time had passed as we researched what was going on. "Yes, he's a friend."

"I know this prick isn't your brother," Kai growls once Lexington loosens his grip slightly. "What the hell is he doing here?"

But the insult instantly tightens Lexington's fingers once more.

"Let him go," I say as the adrenaline subsides in my veins. I turn away from them, folding my arms over my chest and shaking my head. I'm instantly reminded why I needed a break from Kai. "This is Lexington Dawes. He's one of Alivia's House members."

"If I let you go, are you going to keep your mouth shut?" Lexington asks snappily behind me. "About anything you might hear tonight? About our location? About me being here? And generally being an annoying yapper?"

I look over my shoulder, amazed at how even in this tense situation, Lexington still sounds so casual and sarcastic.

The look Kai gives him could kill. His eyes brighten, his big, strong hands tightening on Lexington's. But as strong as Kai is, he's still no match against a Born.

"Kai," I say. "Lexington is here to help. Calm down."

It takes too long, but finally he nods. Lexington releases his death grip on Kai's neck, but keeps the stake pressed to his chest.

"Elle seems to think you're good, which is good enough for me, for the most part," Lexington says. "But I need to hear it from your lips. We good?"

Kai's nostrils flare, breathing in and out hard. His fighting nature is taking hold now. But he nods, looking over at me.

Lexington removes the stake, holding his hands up. But I see the way his shoulders are still tense, the tight grip he keeps on the wood. One wrong move and Lexington will kill him.

"What are you doing here, Kai?" I ask, taking two steps forward, my arms still crossed over my chest.

His eyes search me over, looking for damage, as he always does. "I hadn't heard from you in a few days. I just..." He looks away from me, to Lexington. The look on his face is a mix between disgusted and betrayed. "I got worried after I walked out like that."

"I'm fine," I say simply.

His jaw tightens as he looks away from Lexington back to me. His hands roll into fists and he clenches and loosens them twice.

"Were you really that sick of having me around?" he asks. He stands on the balls of his feet, as if to take a step forward, knowing he shouldn't. "You told me to take the cure, and immediately went and got a replacement?"

I don't like emotions. They complicate and twist things. They take the ease out of everything. They make things messy.

And right now my stomach is in knots. My chest feels tight. And I can't seem to get my lips to move.

I feel another gaze on me and my eyes shift to see Lexington watching me. His expression open, studying. I look back at Kai, but still nothing comes out.

"Looks to me like she doesn't think she needs to explain herself," Lexington pipes up. He takes a step forward, placing himself between Kai and I. "And I don't really know what's going on between the two of you, but it's pretty obvious you don't know everything that's going on here, either."

"The fact that I don't have a clue who you are says a lot, *uso*," Kai says, taking a step forward. "Maybe she needs a friend here more than she needs whoever you are."

"Lexington *is* a friend," I cut in, something in me bristling. And I hate everything about this.

"Look," Lexington says, taking half a step toward Kai. "You obviously care a lot about Elle. Enough to show up unexpectedly in the middle of the night—"

"I was just walking by," Kai says defensively. "I heard a voice inside."

Lexington nods. "I get that. You were just being a good…friend." There's that uncertainty in his voice that a lot of people get when it comes to Kai and me. "But as you can see, she's safe. And I don't know about you, but to me it kind of looks like your current approach is upsetting her."

Kai's eyes dart to mine and I see his expression fall. The distress I don't want to be feeling must be more obvious on my face than I'm trying to let it be.

"We both need some time apart to think," I say evenly. I stare at him, trying so hard to get my message across. "I told you what I think is best. I think that you should take the cure."

He shakes his head. "But then I'm useless. Then I'm just…just some guy again. You don't get to decide what's best for me, Elle."

I take a step forward and Lexington backs up a bit, giving us our space. "Useless is the last thing you would be. A future—a free future, is what you'd have again."

His eyes dart over to Lexington and I know that's all he can see right now: a replacement. And to him, that feels like the ultimate betrayal.

I meet Lexington's eyes. "Can you give us a few minutes?"

I must be learning him quick. I know that look in Lexington's eyes. See the way they search me. An entire conversation happens in just two seconds with not a word spoken. He makes sure I'm okay, and offers a nod. "Sure."

He walks back into the dining room.

He can still hear everything. But at least he's out of sight.

"I'm very sorry if I am hurting you, Kai," I say. It's difficult to meet his eyes. "You've been wonderful to me over these past nine months. But I can't let you keep hoping that something is going to happen. You're my closest friend, but for me…" I shake my head, closing my eyes. I don't want to have to say the words that come out next. "For me that's all it is going to be. And I can't give you the hope that it will change. I have to let you have a life outside of me."

Kai bites the inside of his lower lip, studying me. Trying to see if there's any hesitance to what I'm saying. But he must eventually see that there isn't.

"Okay," he says, his voice broken and defeated. "I'll think about what you've said. You've made it pretty clear you don't feel the same way I feel about you. I guess…I guess I just have to accept that and deal."

My heart sinks. I reach a hand out, intending to touch his shoulder, but he side steps it, and I let my hand fall to my side.

"I'm sorry," I say quietly.

He sniffs hard, nodding his head as he presses his lips tightly together. "Me too," he says. He takes three steps toward the door, reaching for it.

"I need you to be careful," I call out before he can leave. "Vampires, Born and Bitten, are realizing they can do whatever they want without the Allaways punishing them. Things are getting ugly. Please, if you hear of anything, or see anything, let me know."

He looks once more back toward the kitchen where he knows Lexington is. There's a whole argument there on the tip of his tongue. But instead, he just nods.

He walks out the door and shuts it behind him.

I stare at the door, even after I hear Lexington walk back into the living room and lean in the doorway.

"I'd ask you if you were okay, but it's pretty obvious you're not," he says quietly. "So how about we watch a movie to get your mind off of things and then get some sleep?"

I can only stand there for a minute, feeling the muscles in my body slowly relax, one by one. The vice around my throat finally loosens. "That sounds great."

chapter
ELEVEN

I SLIP THROUGH THE AUTOMATIC DOORS, just behind the doctor who has his nose in a chart. Past three doors I slip before hesitating at a corner. Peering around, I find the nurses station just around it.

I look back, meeting Lexington's eyes as he looks through the window in the door I just came through. I tilt my head just a little, pointing to the location of the nurses' station at the same time the only body at it walks in the opposite direction of me.

I only make out a tiny blur and feel the wind rustle my hair as he speeds past me. The faint sound of rustling paper draws my eyes to the station.

In motions I can barely make out, he whips from one chart to the next, searching through records at an insane speed. Finally, a whole seven seconds later, he taps one particular chart.

He darts to my side, grabbing my hand, and tugging me further down the hall. On silent feet, we make our way down, and stop outside of room 216.

A machine beeps inside, bags of blood drip into a tube before slipping into the man's arm.

Lexington closes the door behind us, and I step up to the man's side. His skin is ashy, pale, his lips nearly white. Two puncture wounds on his neck are slowly beginning to heal closed.

His chest rises and falls, gaining speed as I observe him.

"He's turning," I say. I bend over him, pulling one of his eyelids open. A brightening yellow surrounds his pupil.

"Elle, don't!"

But the warning comes a second too late.

The newly awoken Bitten snaps a vice grip hand around my wrist, yanking my arm to his mouth. Newly formed fangs sink into my flesh, and I instantly go numb and still, the blood getting sucked from my arm in deep pulls.

I blink, trying to clear the fog from my brain, I attempt to fight the vampire's toxins.

But not before the fangs are yanked away from my arm. I stumble back, half falling on the floor, half on the bed, as the Bitten goes instantly still. I blink again, my senses coming back to me as I see Lexington pull the needle away.

"You good?" he asks, rushing to my side and helping me to my feet. I stumble once, falling back into his arms, my head lolling to one side just a bit as I blink fast.

"Yeah," I mumble, still recovering. I rest there against his chest for a few moments, finding myself again. "I didn't realize how far along he was."

"I should have reacted faster," Lexington says, supporting me as I climb to my feet. "Sometimes I forget how fearless you are when it comes to us."

I look back at him, and see how genuinely he means it when he makes the statement.

Fearless.

I'd never considered the word applicable to myself.

But he's right, when it comes to vampires, Born or Bitten, it takes a lot to make me afraid of them.

I brace my hands on the bed, looking down at the man who now lies there so still. It all happened so quick, he immediately dropped into unconsciousness. He didn't even have to go through the pain.

"Can you imagine if we'd gotten here even two minutes later?" I say quietly, watching as the man's features relax slowly. "He would have woken up, grabbed the first person he could have found, and drained them. He would have exposed himself to the whole hospital."

"The Allaways hands-off approach is going to get all of us exposed real quick here," Lexington says as he rubs his hand over my back, not quite ready to let me stand on my own two feet.

I nod.

In the past four weeks that we've been tracking the news and listening to police scanners, there's been another twelve attacks. Over half a dozen online magazines have started talking about the mysterious "animal attacks" that are happening all over the North East.

This is getting out of hand.

"I'm tired," I say, standing straight, feeling my shoulders sag. Lexington immediately steps up, his hands on my shoulders.

"You need me to carry you back home?" he asks quietly, his lips near my ear.

I shake my head. "I mean I'm exhausted holding all this. Knowing what's happening here, what might come. And feeling like I can't do near enough about it. These are real people, Lexington. They're all innocent. And Charles is doing nothing to protect them."

He turns me in his arms, pulling me into his chest. And it's the most comforting gesture I think I've felt in a very long time.

I don't speak the honest truth very often. Don't expose what's really on the inside when I'm feeling weak. I've stood on my own for so long now. Held myself together. Did everything on my own.

But in just four weeks, I've come to lean on this man. Come to crave the strength he offers.

"We need to call Liv," Lexington says gently into my ear. "We need to make a real plan. And I think we need to consider tattling."

"What do you mean?" I ask, my brows furrowing as I look up into his blue eyes.

"I mean," he says, tucking a lock of hair behind my ear. "I think we need to consider alerting Cyrus that Charles is failing at his job."

I shake my head. "Are you crazy?" I take a step back. "The last time he came to the States he had my brother sent to prison for months. He scared Liv into taking her own life. Everything takes a turn for the dark when he's around, Lexington."

He nods his head. "I know," he says, pushing his hands into his pockets. He hovers on the balls of his feet, like he very much wants to take some kind of action right now. "But Elle, you said it yourself, taking this all on ourselves, just the two of us, it's exhausting. And it's not near enough."

A noise out in the hall catches my attention, and the next second, Lexington has hauled the two of us into the corner behind the door. It swings open, hiding our location. I hold my breath, nearly impossible to do with my pulse racing like it is. I stand as still as possible, pressed up against Lexington's back.

A nurse checks the patient's blood pressure, notes his heart rate. Generally fusses over his state. It feels like it takes forever before she finally leaves, closing the door behind her.

I let out a big breath, stepping out from the corner.

"I just think ..." I say, my mind reeling as I go over every implication of this situation. "I just think we should talk to Liv and Ian first. We've got to come up with some kind of solution first before we have to resort to involving Cyrus."

"Yeah," he says, offering me a little smile. "I don't want to bring him over either. Let's head home and give them a call."

It can't really be that easy to convince him to try my way. If this were Ian, it would be a huge fight that would dramatically last over several days, with him being angry and annoyed the entire time.

But as the two of us sneak out of the hospital room, I kind of think it really is this easy.

We walk toward the subway out in front of the hospital and just before we walk down into the tunnel, I look up at the gray skies above us that threaten snow.

Stormy skies freak me out.

Curses. People dying. Threats to my family.

I can't even imagine what a normal life would be like.

All because several thousand years ago, a man became obsessed with his own immortality.

Cyrus was as much of a scientist as there ever had been, long, long ago. He created a serum, which made him immortal and gave him insane strength and speed. The ultimate hunter.

He had a wife, whom he loved more than anything in the world, and he wanted her to join him in immortality. The stories say she refused, she was terrified of what her husband had become.

In the end, Cyrus forced it upon her.

Little did he know she was pregnant with their child.

Sevan gained immortality too, all the same strengths and speed. A few months later she gave birth to a son.

In the beginning he seemed perfectly human. Normal. For years he grew and aged. He ate food just like any other human, unlike his cursed parents who now craved the blood of what they once were.

The child however, died when he was eighteen years old.

Cyrus and Sevan buried him. Mourned him.

But four days later, he clawed his way out of that grave, Resurrected. His thirst was immense, and his eyes matched his parents. He just had to taste death first.

A few years later, a woman the son had laid with conceived and gave birth to a baby boy. When at a grown age, the son killed Cyrus' grandson to see if he had been granted the same curse. He Resurrected as well.

Over the next few decades, the son created more children, killing each of them when they reached adulthood. The ideas of power and domination they could inflict dominated the son's thoughts.

But Cyrus valued secrecy over all else. He knew the dangers of taking on more than they could handle.

A war broke out. The son, with five of his seven sons, against Cyrus, and two of his grandsons.

Cyrus won. He eliminated his son, and killed or banished the five who rebelled. And he gave everything to his two grandsons who remained loyal to him. Money, power, charge over the world. They and their descendants were Royals, and to this day, it is they and their posterity who rule the Houses.

Dorian and Malachi, the third and seventh son.

I met both of them when Cyrus kidnapped me and took me to Roter Himmel, where the King lives in Austria, to serve as judge for Alivia's trial. Alivia is a direct descendent of Dorian.

The rest of the Born are descendants of one of the other five sons. As physically strong and capable as the Royals, but with no esteem or grace in the King's eyes. No rights to leadership or rule. No claim to any of the King's immense wealth.

Like Lexington.

Like Ian.

The Royals are a big deal.

Alivia was an even bigger deal, because when she was discovered, it rocked a very big boat.

My sister-in-law was once a normal girl, born to a single mother in Colorado. Her mother was from Mississippi, where she met Henry Conrath, a Royal who walked away from King Cyrus' political system after his brother had been killed for something he didn't do. Alivia's mother moved to Colorado, having no idea what Henry was, where she raised Alivia on her own, not telling Henry about the child until Alivia was grown.

She had no idea who her father was, until she received a will in the mail, stating Henry had just died and left her everything, including his massive estate in Mississippi.

By this point Alivia's mother had been killed in an accident, and with nothing stopping her, she moved to Mississippi, having no idea what she'd find there, or even what she truly was.

Cue a lot of secrets, chaos, lots of dramatics. After nearly killing her, my brother fell in love with her, before he knew he himself was a Born, that our mother had an affair. Him falling in love with Alivia got him killed by one of her enemies who wanted her throne. Four days later my brother woke up in a grave, craving blood.

In the end, Alivia found her rightful place, fighting against a lot of people who didn't want her on the throne. She and my brother got over themselves and just decided to love each other, and now they've been happily married for six years.

I shake my head as I watch the lights flash by on the subway.

It's all so insane. So big and fantastical and dark.

How is this my real life?

Lexington and I get off the subway and finish walking the last two blocks to my apartment. On the stairs waits a package, one marked as coming from Arizona. But I know it's not really from Arizona, and I know it's from Henry, containing more doses of the Bitten cure.

I pull my coat off when we walk into my living room, and realize there's blood smeared all over it where the Bitten bit me.

"Whoa," Lexington says, as his eyes instantly fix on it. And for just a second, red flashes in his eyes.

I have to remember that he is in fact a Born, and he does always crave my blood.

"Sit there," he says, pulling his own coat off, instantly back in control. "I'll get something to clean that up."

I don't want to sit. I don't want to look at my own blood. What I want right now is to go up to my garden and pretend that all I need to worry about is the fact that winter is here and nothing more will be growing until spring.

But just a moment later, Lexington returns with a wet washcloth and a first aid kit.

"I'm sorry, again," he says as he directs me to sit on the couch and he sits on the coffee table. He pulls my hand into his lap and begins cleaning my arm. "I heard his breathing and reacted just a second too late."

"It's okay," I say quietly, not really seeing the blood smear all over my arm.

"Not really," he says with a sigh. He wipes the last of the blood away, and just stares at my arm for a minute. "I said you were fearless, and I guess I now see why. Any fear has been sucked out of you, little by little."

He touches his fingers lightly to one set of scars, half circles, and then the other. His touch is gentle, soft, reverent.

Lexington reaches for my other hand, setting it beside the other. He pulls my sleeve up, revealing another set of identical scars. With one addition.

A faint white cross is etched into my skin there.

"Elle, how the hell are you even still alive?" Lexington breathes as he studies the scars there.

I shrug, trying so very hard to gather the numbness I'm so good at hiding in. "I've learned to adapt. To just keep surviving."

Lexington shakes his head, and I look up to see the pain in his expression. "How many times have you been fed off of?"

"Once by Henry," I say, losing my grip on the numbness. "Twice by Trinity, but don't tell Liv that." I hurry to say that when the shock takes over Lexington's face. "Markov has tried three times, but you know about most of those."

Lexington himself is the one who removed me from being drained once.

"And today marks the twenty-sixth Bitten who's sunk their fangs into me," I finish. The twenty-sixth time I've suddenly frozen still, my mind fogging over. I'm helpless when they bite me.

And suddenly I realize just how much of a miracle it truly is that I'm still alive. Or not a Bitten myself.

"And this one?" Lexington asks, tracing his finger down the center of the cross.

I pull my arms away from him suddenly. The familiar feeling of shame begins clawing it's way up my chest like a startled spider.

"Elle," Lexington says, his voice breathy. "Who the hell did that to you?"

I can't seem to meet his eyes. They fix on a framed picture of Ian, Lula, and I that hangs on the wall. "There's a reason why I haven't gone back to Silent Bend. Why, once Lula was dead, I finally felt free of that place and the people there."

I finally look back at Lexington. His eyes are the most serious I've ever seen. He leans, slightly inclined toward me. His hands reach back out, and I let him take both of mine in his.

The way he's looking at me, it opens a little crack in my chest. It causes the breath to hitch in my throat.

Something bites at the back of my eyes.

"Yet you're not broken, Elle," he says quietly. He leans forward, and he brings one of his hands up to the back of my neck as he touches his forehead to mine. "You're a fighter, one of the strongest, bravest people I've seen. People might look at you and assume otherwise. But I know what you are, Elle. Fearless."

I sniff, holding in the tears that threaten to break free.

I don't cry.

I don't need to.

But Lexington brings out emotion in me. And I think I need to allow that to happen every now and then.

"Thank you," I breathe.

He nods, and I take in his scent, fully enveloped in the moment.

Until the laptop in the dining room sounds off with an incoming call.

"I got this," he says. He backs away.

Instantly, I can breathe again. But instantly, I feel cold.

"Were your ears ringing?" I hear Lexington joke from the dining room. Faintly, I hear Ian and Liv's voices.

My limbs are somewhat numb as I stand. I pull my sleeves down over my arms and head into the dining room.

"Are you two on one of those freaky sibling wave lengths?" Lexington jokes as I sit in a chair beside him. But it's forced. I see the look in his eyes, and he's trying too hard to help me not let them see how affected I am right now.

"What's wrong?" Ian instantly asks though, his face going serious and stern on the screen. Even Alivia's brows furrow.

"I'm fine," I say, instantly feeling like the little girl again under the protection of her big brother.

"No you're not," he says, calling me out. My brother has never been one to beat around the bush. "And why the hell are *you* looking at her like that?"

Lexington leans back away form the computer. "Like what?" he scoffs.

"You keep your damn hands off of my sister, Lex, or I swear—"

"Knock it off, Ian," I cut him off. "Seriously, you have to stop doing that."

"You know that's never going to happen," he says, still glaring. Lexington looks over at me, his expression just slightly sheepish. "But seriously, what's wrong?"

Instead of answering him, I slide the laptop back on the table, widening its view, and tilt it upwards. The camera gives them a clear view of the map that hangs on the wall. "Things aren't going so well up here."

"Each of those dots represents a blatantly obvious vampire attack," Lexington jumps in to explain. "This is just in the last seven months."

"They're all centered around Charles' House," Alivia observes, staring closely at the screen. "What about the last year? The last two years?"

"There haven't been as many attacks," I say, looking over at Lexington for confirmation. "They've definitely been picking up speed in the recent months."

"The vamps in this area are starting to realize they no longer have to answer to anyone," Lexington says, setting his arm across the back of my chair. "Things are starting to get out of hand, and fear is starting to spread."

"The fact that some of us have fangs isn't going to stay hidden for long," Ian concludes. "Have you heard any word of this from anyone at Court?"

Alivia shakes her head. "It's been a while since I've talked to anyone from *Roter Himmel* though."

"Has there been any contact with Charles in the last few weeks?" Lexington asks.

Alivia shakes her head. "Not directly through either of us. But Trinity and Christian both received letters with checks for a very large amount as a bribe to join his House."

"He's still trying to buy members," I say. "Did either of them accept?"

"No," she says, leaning back in her chair and propping one foot up on it. "But if he's still trying this hard with *our* House, I can only imagine the pressure he's putting on the other Houses."

"Well, at this point I'd say maybe we need to help in the cause," Lexington says, folding his arms on the table. "He needs some numbers to help get things back under control."

Ian shakes his head. "I don't think you realize just what a laughing stock he is to the Houses right now. No one trusts him. No one is willing to take the risk that they'll be knocked off like his sister was, and all those other House members."

"But that threat has been eliminated," I say. It was my own mother who had them all killed. And she's dead now.

Alivia shrugs. "It takes vampires a long time to get over things and forget."

Lexington shrugs. "Then why don't you guys come up here and knock him off the throne? You've done a pretty bang up job keeping things under control in the South."

Alivia laughs. "I'm barely keeping a grasp on everything here. Suddenly expanding the rule of the House of Conrath to half the country? No thanks."

"You said there were rumors about Cyrus sending hunters and making an enquiry," I say. "Anything happening with that?"

Alivia shakes her head. "No one has come around here wanting to talk. Yet. But Danny found three dead Bitten in Jackson about two weeks ago."

"The whole world's going deadly," Lexington says.

"I'm not worried about things down here, we'll handle it," Ian says. "But things up there are a problem."

"So, what?" Lexington says. "What are our options? I don't know what else to do other than flag down Cyrus and tell him he needs to instate a new Royal."

"And who knows what else will happen when he comes across the ocean," Ian says as he rolls his eyes. "You obviously haven't spent enough time around the maniac if you're suggesting we turn to *Cyrus* for help."

"Give us some options here," I say, jumping in, because when Ian goes back to dark memories, it doesn't go well for anyone. "We've been doing everything we can for the past few weeks, but this is too big for just the two of us to handle."

Ian's expression instantly grows darker, if that's possible. "Do I need to haul you into some deep, dark cave and lock you up? I haven't been protecting you for the past twenty-three years for you to go gallivanting around, playing vigilante."

"Your sister's been doing a damn fine job keeping the Bitten in check," Lexington pipes up, leaning forward, as if challenging Ian through the computer screen. "You've been doing this forever, bro. It's time to realize your baby sister isn't a baby anymore."

Ian lunges toward the screen, his expression full of rage. Alivia's hands dart out though, pulling him back. He still glares death as he meets Lexington's eyes. "Knew I should have sent Leigh instead of you."

"Really, Ian?" Alivia says, annoyance in her voice. "You know he's right. Elle's been doing just fine. You need to give her a little more credit. She's a college graduate, a successful businesswoman. You need to realize by now she can take care of herself."

I can't handle this. The same argument that's been had over so many years. I get up from the table and head to the living room.

Shada darts down the stairs, rubbing her head over my ankles until I pick her up. Quietly, I hear Ian and Lexington arguing.

I open the front door, walk down the stairs, through the foyer, and step out onto the front porch, sitting on the top stair.

The neighborhood is fairly quiet. Rows of Victorian row homes line the street, each of them costing a pretty penny. If you want to live in Back Bay, you're going to have to fork out a lot of cash if you don't inherit a place that's been passed down for generations.

I watch as a couple jogs down the road, puffs of condensation billowing into the cold air. An old man helps his aged wife up the stairs across the road, walking slowly and careful not to slip.

I feel the temperature drop. The weather said it's supposed to snow on Monday.

Movement down the road pulls my eyes to the right. A police car rolls down the street, before taking a left, heading in another direction to patrol the streets.

A light goes off in my head. I scramble to my feet, darting back inside. When I walk into the dining room, Lexington and Ian are still going at it, Alivia trying to play referee.

"We need a sheriff, of sorts," I blurt out, interrupting their annoying quarrel.

"What?" Ian asks, struggling to catch up to the change of direction.

"Or rather, we need…a stand in. You two can't come up here to get everything under control, not without the threat of starting a war with Charles," I say as I place my hands on my hips, my mind racing. "And yes, you could beat him if it came to that, but that's just going to draw more attention, which no one wants. And you can't really send any more of your people up here without drawing some of that as well."

"What are you suggesting?" Alivia asks.

"Lexington knows how the Houses work, he's been around long enough, he knows how things should be done to keep things under control," I say, looking at him. His expression is unreadable, but open. "But him trying to take charge is going to be seen as an act of war too, considering the House of Allaway gave him up six years ago. What we need is someone to be the face of accountability until Charles gets his crap together. Someone these vampires have to answer to. Someone to be—"

"Our puppet?" he asks, sounding incredibly unsure.

"Sort of," I say. My mind is flipping through all of the different Born I've met over the years, searching for the right solution. "They'll dole out punishment to those who get out of line, put the fear back in them. And maybe…"

"Maybe we can start up a mock House," Lexington suddenly says, excitement building in his voice. I meet his eyes, nodding. "Sort of like Jasmine did before you came to town, Liv. You've got to admit, she did set the ground roots for you building your House."

Alivia nods. "She may have hated me from the moment I stepped foot into town, but she did make it easier to start my House. I still have almost every member she recruited."

"I've got to admit, it's a good plan," Ian says, looking over at Alivia, who nods in agreement. "Never thought mimicking Jasmine Voltera would be something we'd resort to. Though it might take some time to take effect. I worry we don't have that kind of time before we all get exposed."

"We'll keep doing what we've been doing," Lexington says, looking at me for confirmation. I'm tired. I want to go back to my shop and my semi-normal life I've carved out for myself.

But this is too big. Too important for me to walk away from.

"Yeah," I agree.

"So," Alivia says. "Anybody got someone like Jasmine in mind?"

"Actually, yeah," Lexington says, realization dawning in his eyes. "I think I do."

chapter TWELVE

"A ND WHAT'S IN IT FOR us?" the woman says, leaning forward and stirring the straw in her black coffee.

Lexington leans forward, rubbing his hands together in his lap. "You get to boss people around, kick some ass."

"I like the sound of that," she says, a lopsided smile pulling at one side of her face.

"And *you* may end up with some company other than that of this fine ray of sunshine," Lexington says to the man sitting beside her.

Lexington and I sit in a coffee shop in Brooklyn at a table, across from Aleah and Duncan Steele. I can faintly tell they are cousins, but so far, their personalities are vastly different.

Aleah: who wears dark, heavy eye make up and always a bitter expression on her face looks to be around twenty, maybe twenty-one. She's fairly tall, taller than me, but she's rail thin. A wide mouth and a narrow nose make for a beautiful face. But her countenance and appearance are very off-putting. She wears a gray jacket, the hood pulled up, and black pants which tuck into thick black boots.

She does in fact look ready to kick some ass.

But her cousin sits there in his black and white striped shirt with his black sweater. He wears neat jeans and a pair of very clean and fresh looking white sneakers. Duncan very much looks the academic type. He's barely said more than five words this entire time. I'd guess he's around twenty, as well.

"Besides the power, the House of Conrath is willing to front rent on a place closer to us, some place big enough to house whoever might want to join in the cause," Lexington continues on. "We've already found a nice place in Cambridge."

"Cambridge," Aleah chuckles with a sneer. "It's a far cry from Brooklyn."

"Well, you might miss the nightly shootings, the drug deals, and the smell," Lexington says, giving her a look. "But hey, Harvard isn't too shabby."

"You really mean it that you have something that will let us walk around during the day again?" Duncan asks, leaning forward, brushing away the banter.

"We'll see how things go first," Lexington says. Everything about his body language says he doesn't trust these two yet, and I'm still trying to figure out why he reached out to them. "Help us out. If things go as hoped, we'll make an upgrade to your status. That includes more than just the ability to walk out in the day."

He means money. Financial support from the House of Conrath.

Duncan's eyes widen slightly and he looks over to Aleah. It's pretty clear. She's the one in charge.

"It seems too good to be true," she says. "Why aren't you the one doing this? You're the one with all the experience with the Houses. You know I don't play well with others."

"I've got other responsibilities at the moment," Lexington says, and I feel him shift just slightly closer to me. "And that's why I'm proposing this to the *two* of you. You can deal with those who don't want to cooperate and obey the rules, and you're persuasive when you want to be in getting others to do what you want them to."

She smiles at that.

"And your cousin here knows how to deal with people." Lexington looks from her to him. "I'll always be available to help where needed."

Aleah's eyes slide from Lexington to me. "She hasn't said more than two words this whole time, but she's obviously someone important. She's the reason you're not setting us up right in the city with you, isn't she?"

"Maybe," Lexington says, his eyes darkening. "But I highly suggest you don't look too closely at her."

But Aleah does look me over, sizing me up, trying to peel away my layers and discover what's underneath. "Yeah, she's someone important. You won't even tell us her name. She must be connected to one of the families."

"Just, leave it, Aleah," Duncan says, annoyance in his voice. "Lexington is offering us a good deal here. We're never going to get a chance like this again. Take it."

Aleah stares Lexington down, mulling everything over. Her gaze is so penetrating and intimidating. "Fine," she says. "I'll do it on a trial basis. If I don't like it, I walk without a word. We'll be there tomorrow night."

Without a word, she stands and walks to the door.

"Thank you," Duncan says, scrambling to gather his things and follow his cousin out the door. "Well get in touch tomorrow."

Lexington nods, a thin-lipped smile on his face as he watches them go.

"They're an interesting pair," I say as I watch the door swing closed.

"They're about as good as we're going to get on such short notice," Lexington says as we rise and head outside. The cousins are nowhere to be seen.

"So what's their story?" I ask as we head to the car Lexington bought over the weekend. He holds the passenger door open for me and I climb in. The second he starts the engine I blast the heat.

A three-inch deep layer of snow lines the ground from the storm that blew through three days ago.

"So, the Steele family was a big one, from New York for forever and ever," Lexington says as he pulls out on to the road and with the guidance of the GPS on his phone, points us in the direction of home. "Not sure which of the five exiled brothers their family stemmed from, but a long time ago they ended up here in the States."

I look outside, at the huge city that surrounds us. I took a train through New York on my trip back east, but was too intimidated to get off and explore.

"I think there were something like four original Steele brothers, and they each had a bunch of kids," he continues. "I think there were something like thirty-five cousins as of twenty years ago."

"That's basically a House," I say in shock. "Do they all live in Brooklyn?"

Lexington shakes his head. "Aleah and Duncan are the only ones left. One night, one of the four brothers went crazy. He went all around the city and killed every one of them. Except Aleah. She realized what was going on, and she put a stop to it."

"She killed her uncle," I fill in the blanks.

Lexington nods. "She has no idea why he murdered the entire family, put a stake through every one of their hearts. The only reason Duncan is still alive is because he was actually going to night university, he was away at school. But as soon as he found out what had happened to his family, he came back to be with the last family member he had left. His cousin."

"That's awful," I say, shaking my head. "I can only imagine what they went through."

Lexington nods once more. "There's a reason Aleah is so unpleasant. She was never the nicest before the massacre, but after…"

It's understandable. Anyone would be angry. And she may never get any answers as to why he killed them all.

"So the Steele family has no ties to Charles?" I ask.

"No need, really," Lexington says. "They had such a large family they didn't need to join a House. Like I said, you join a House for companionship or protection, or both. They didn't need either with a family that big."

It's perfect. They have nothing against Charles, and Aleah's not going to be afraid of someone coming after her if she ever decides to join his House. She's already survived a horrific attack and was the one to put an end to it.

"How did you meet them?" I ask.

"Duncan is a pretty smart guy," Lexington says as he rubs two fingers over his lips. "He'd been trying to do some research on his family roots about nine years ago. He reached out to the Allaways to see if they knew anything, and they sent him to me. I helped him do some research and wherever one cousin goes, the other does too, now."

"Were you able to help him find what he was looking for?"

Lexington shakes his head. "We got back as far as 1581, but the trail went cold there."

I nod. There are so many deep roots in this world, so many hidden paths and family ties. Such a complex world.

"Do you think this is going to work?" I say quietly as I rest my forehead against the cold glass.

"It has to," Lexington says as he reaches over and takes my hand in his.

chapter
THIRTEEN

B LOOD COATS MY FEET, STAINING my white shoes as I walk across an open field. Body after body blocks my way, so many innocent, so many dead. Screams and shouts are a chorus that electrifies the air.

Cold metal sucks all the warmth from my fingers. The scent of gunpowder and steel stings my nose.

Words echo across the field. Words that cut me to the core. Words that tear me into pieces and leave me a shredded mess on the ground.

I level the rifle to my eye. I take aim.

I pull the trigger.

Blood explodes from my mother's chest, and she sags forward.

Dead.

With a gasp, I startle from sleep, sitting up in my bed, expecting to find bodies littering the ground around me.

But there's only a dark room, and Cora is nowhere to be seen.

I lay back in my bed, staring at the ceiling as my heart rate settles back down, ever so slowly.

It's a nightmare that visits me frequently. Replaying the one and only memory I have of the woman who gave birth to me, over and over.

Without giving it permission, my mind immediately goes back to that day. To the bodies and the deaths and all the blood. So many innocent. So many that I had known, losing their lives.

My mind races through every detail, recalling every horrifying minute.

I swing my legs off the side of the bed and climb out.

Once my brain goes to that night, it's hard to escape, and there's already enough darkness in my heart, I can't have more tonight.

I quietly pad down the stairs, hoping to not wake Lexington if he's sleeping. I round into the kitchen, opening the fridge to get some milk.

"You okay?"

I startle slightly, turning to faintly make out Lexington's face at the dining table, illuminated by the glow of his computer screen.

"Yeah," I say, pulling out the carton and filling a glass. "Just…a nightmare." For some reason, I always confess the truth to him, when I've hardly ever done that with anyone else.

"Thankfully we usually wake up from those," he says quietly as he watches me cross the kitchen and sit in the chair beside him.

"Usually," I say as I tuck my knees up to my chest and hold the glass between my hands on the table. "What are you working on?"

Lexington shrugs, looking back to his screen. "Just the usual maintenance stuff."

"What's that supposed to mean?" I study his face in the dim light, noticing the stubble that's growing back from when he shaved yesterday.

He chuckles, rubbing a hand over the back of his neck. "I wouldn't say I have a job, but I do have investments I've made over the years that I still have to keep an eye on."

I nod. I guess I should have thought Lexington would have a way to provide for himself financially, but I didn't. "You really enjoy doing stuff on the computer, don't you?"

He looks over at me and smiles. "I guess they seemed like magic, back when I first started hearing about them. The possibilities just seemed so endless. I uh... I bought stock in this one company, early on. Let's just say it was a wise move, but looked real risky at the time."

"Are you trying to tell me you're rich or something?" I say with a little smile.

Lexington shrugs. "I wouldn't call it rich, but I promise I'm not just mooching a free place to live off of you."

I chuckle, shaking my head. "So is this what you do every night when I'm sleeping?"

Lexington leans back, his eyes going back to his computer screen. "Pretty much. I mean, I've been digging around Charles, but there's not much to find. He's been real quiet these days. But yeah, the computer keeps me occupied while you're snoozing away." He smiles. "Though I will say that I think I sleep more than your average vampire."

Of course he does. It's so fitting that the relaxed, casual vampire is the one who can take it easy enough to sleep.

"You should tell me about your time living with Charles," I say, taking a sip from my cup. "Did you like living with the Allaways?"

Lexington shrugs. "At the time, I thought I did. I mean, I'd been alone for a long time before that, so mostly it was nice to have company all the time. And the parties…"

"Charles liked parties?"

Lexington smiles and shakes his head. "It was mostly Chelsea. Anything that brought her attention, put her in the spotlight. She and Charles would always come up with the most ridiculous outfits, and they always matched. I don't think they realized how weird that was."

I smile, watching Lexington light up as he recounts his past. I realize now how little I know about his very long history.

"It was easy to kind of forget who you were as a person in that House," he continues, looking off into nothing. "I mean, it was a party every other weekend, but during the week, it was all about acting the part of a Royal too. See, everyone is still productive at Liv's House, but in the Allaways… we sat around and let others do the dirty work for us."

"So Charles has never really had to work for anything," I say.

Lexington nods. "He cared about his friends, his dog, and his sister. Not much else ever bothered him."

"Sounds like you were a different person back then," I say quietly, looking at him.

His eyes slide over to me and there's a little bit of shame in them maybe. "I was. I guess I just got caught up in their way of thinking, I got kind of entitled and lazy. I wasn't like that before I joined their House, and I haven't been like that since they gave me away."

"People can always change," I say, holding his gaze. "If they want to."

"Yeah," he says quietly. "I just hope it continues to be for the better."

chapter

FOURTEEN

I PACE IN THE FRONT ROOM of the house Alivia rented for our plan. The clock ticks toward one o'clock.

"It's been dark for five hours," I say. "It only takes four and a half to drive here."

"They're from Brooklyn," Lexington says. "Trust me, they don't have their own car. They're taking the bus."

I nod. Having to make use of public transportation is something I'm still getting used to, even though I haven't had my own car in two years now.

Finally, I perch on the edge of the couch, staring at the front door.

Lexington tries to distract me by telling me stories about himself from the twenties. About prohibition, traveling to the wild west of Arizona. How he tried Chinese food for the first time in Chicago.

I'm genuinely interested, but when anticipation and anxiety work their way into my system, I have a really hard time focusing on anything else.

An hour later, I hear noises out on the front porch. A second later, Aleah shoves her way through the front door, three large bags over her shoulders.

"You just going to sit there uselessly?" she snaps at me the second our eyes meet. I scramble to my feet, taking two of the bags from her. A moment after she steps inside, Duncan follows her in, carrying five bags.

Aleah drops her stuff on the ground and looks around the space.

High ceilings, wood trim, and white accents are splashed around the house. The large living room cuts off the hall of the entryway, leading back into a grand kitchen, spacious dining room, and an even bigger great room. Upstairs there are five bedrooms and an office.

I can only imagine the fortune it's costing the House of Conrath, when this shouldn't be their problem.

"Fancy place," Aleah says, stalking through the hall, leaving a trail of slightly muddy boot prints behind her. Duncan shakes his head at her, but follows behind.

She immediately goes to the fridge, which I stocked with a few basics. She takes out a blood bag from the top shelf. "You know I don't drink this stuff, right?" she says, giving Lexington a look.

"I do now," he says, giving her a somewhat annoyed smile. "But you remember your entire purpose here is to keep the secret from coming to light, right?"

"Please," she says with a smile as she tosses the bag to Duncan, who does pop it open for a drink. "My very large family managed to live in

New York undetected for over two hundred years. I know how to take my dinner without being noticed."

She walks past me, her eyes trained on me the whole time. "Though I don't know how you manage to spend twenty-four-seven with this one and not take a little sample. She smells like dessert."

I take half a step away from Aleah as she gives me a dark smile and heads up the stairs.

"Don't listen to my cousin," Duncan says, tossing the empty blood bag into the garbage. "Getting under people's skin is just a game to her."

"One I'm sure she's pretty good at," I say.

"Most of the time," he says. He crosses back into the living room and opens his backpack. He pulls out a laptop and goes back to the dining table. Instantly, he starts clicking away on it.

"This place will work," Aleah says, suddenly jumping over the railing and landing on the wood floors loudly, I'm sure just to make me jump. "The rules are that if I catch anyone being reckless you don't get to dictate what the punishment is."

She holds the edges of her leather jacket, looking very deadly and dangerous in such a beautiful and historical setting.

"So long as you're discreet," Lexington says. The look in his eyes says he knows he's involved a weapon he can't really control.

"We're going to have to start this out with a bang, you know that, right?" she says as a smile starts forming on her face. "We're not going to get anyone's attention without making an example."

"Do what you've got to do," he says.

The smile fully forms on her face. She turns on her heel and walks back toward the front door. "I'll check in every now and then, but I expect not to feel like I'm being babysat." She stops in the doorway, looking back at us. "Let me do the job you recruited me for."

With that, she walks out and slams the door behind her.

"And that's my cousin," Duncan says with the raise of an eyebrow.

chapter
FIFTEEN

I'M NOT SURE WHAT ALEAH does to make her example, but within a week she gets some guy named Robert to move into the house and join her in putting the New England area back in order. I try to avoid her as much as possible, and thankfully I only have to see her once in that first week.

Lexington gets texts from her frequently. Usually one or two word messages, but she's effective in her job. She takes out three attackers in the first seven days.

She's effective considering she's limited to the night-dark hours of the day.

A week before Christmas, I stand in my lab, maybe sort of feeling like I've kind of gotten back to my normal life. Snow softly falls outside. Customers have been coming and going all day. I've completely sold out of the Adore Me love perfume. Half the men in this city seem to think it's the perfect Christmas gift. And I'm not feeling guilty being here, like I should be out fighting crimes committed by vampires.

Lexington isn't even here. He's out helping Duncan with something.

All that's missing is Kai, waiting to step in and ask if he can walk me home. But that doesn't happen anymore. I haven't heard from him in two weeks, and the only word I did get was a text asking if everything was going okay.

It breaks my heart to lose a friend like that when all I tried to do was tell him the truth. But it's better this way. I had to do what was best for the both of us.

Rose petals, hawthorn berries, chamomile, and lavender are spread out over the counters as I mix up a tea blend for a woman who came in begging for a solution to her teething baby who had been crying for three days straight.

I scoop out a tablespoon of honey and add it to the saucepan on the burner. I stir the mixture, bringing it to a simmer.

The computer dings from the corner, and after turning the heat off, I check it.

Another email from Rose. This time asking for a new recipe, one that calls for ingredients like wolfsbane, vervain, and willow bark.

I press my lips together, staring at her name at the top of the email.

I don't want to keep working with Rose. Her requests scare me, her very presence makes me want to crawl right out of my own skin. And I can't find logical, sound explanations for the things she asks me to make.

Nothing about Rose is normal. But I'm certain she isn't a vampire.

That's as far as my realm of knowledge extends.

I don't have a desire for it to reach any further.

The bell above the door in the shop rings and I flinch slightly, startled. I step to the side to go help the customer, and bump straight into Lexington. Instantly, I'm reaching for the stake in my back pocket.

"Whoa, there," he says, his hand snapping to stop me from pulling it free. "Just me."

"Sorry," I say, forcing my pulse to relax. I turn back to the baby's drink, and pour it into a glass bottle. "I wasn't expecting you back so soon."

"Considering I'm not supposed to be gone at all, I thought I better not take too long."

"Not like anything has happened," I say, feeling irritated and impatient. "It's been a month and a half, and there's not been a word from Charles Allaway. I'm beginning to think Ian was just overreacting, as usual."

"Or maybe that just means I'm doing my job well?" Lexington says, a hint of offense in his voice. "I would think you of all people would know that even if you don't see it right in front of your face, that doesn't mean the threat isn't there in the shadows."

"Don't bring my mother into this," I hiss, wielding the spatula in his direction.

"Sorry," he says, throwing his hands up in surrender, taking a step back. The look on his face is confused, hurt.

I'm freaking out on him, and he doesn't deserve it.

And I'm not entirely sure why I'm feeling this way.

A blinking red light starts flashing from one wall. The one that only goes off every so often lately.

"Looks like you've got a visitor," Lexington says, nodding his head toward it.

I cork the bottle and head into the shop. Gray clouds darken the late afternoon. With only ten minutes until closing time, I lock the front door and turn the sign over to CLOSED.

"Come on," I say, not quite meeting Lexington's eyes.

We step through the hidden door and he leads the way down the stairs and through the hall. He pushes the door open and we both step in.

Kai stands inside, holding back a very large man who immediately snaps in my direction the second I step inside.

"Kai," I say in shock. "What… what are you doing here?"

He fixes me with his dark eyes, so much conflict there. "I was walking home last night when I heard the yell. It was another Bitten who attacked this guy. I couldn't get him under control."

I know what that means. Kai had to eliminate him.

"I didn't dare take him to the hospital," Kai says. The man suddenly lunges toward me and Lexington darts forward. The man is instantly on the ground, Lexington's knee in his back, his hand forcing his face down into the stone floor. "He turned about an hour ago."

"Okay," I nod, still in shock that Kai is here again. Almost like the last two months haven't passed.

I cross to the opposite wall, swinging aside the painting to reveal the keypad. I enter the code, and the hidden panel pops open. I pull on some gloves and remove a needle. "This is going to hurt for about a minute," I begin explaining. I turn, crouching beside the man while Lexington easily keeps him from killing me. "I know you're starving right now and all you can think about is draining me. But this will put you back to normal."

I sink the needle into his meaty shoulder, and the moment I remove it, the man bellows in pain. His body curls into the fetal position, his hands shaking violently. Lexington backs off of him, but doesn't stand, just in case he needs to contain the man.

He won't. The poor man is in too much pain for that.

I turn away from him, unable to watch an individual in so much pain. I put the needle into the sharps container and throw my gloves in the garbage. I lock the fridge back up. I face the wall for a moment, rubbing one hand over my forearm.

"He's good," Lexington says. I look over my shoulder to see the man finally fall still. Kai grabs his wrists and hauls him over to the cot.

"How have you been?" I ask, even though I can't fully meet Kai's eyes.

"I've had a lot of thinking to do," he says. "But it's been good."

"Really?" I ask, my eyes rising up to his.

Lexington awkwardly backs up into a corner, trying to give us a little bit of privacy in this very small room.

Kai looks sideways at him, but he knows he's not going anywhere. He's just going to have to make do.

"I didn't like what you had to say, but I guess some time to process it just let me realize you did and said what you thought was best."

"I didn't do it to hurt you," I say, shaking my head.

The look in his eyes says that I did hurt him, but he realizes now that wasn't my intent. "You may not feel the same way I did, and that hurt, but it's better I knew earlier."

"The way you *did*?" I ask for clarification.

He shrugs. "Like I said, I had a lot of time to think. You were right, I let you occupy every minute. As *tina* pointed out, that's just obsession. So, I uh…went on a few dates."

This pulls a little smile on my lips. "I'm happy to hear that. You need to do things for you."

He nods his head. "It made me realize that we might not evolve into what I hoped, but you're still one of my best friends, Elle. You're still family."

The smile finally forms on my lips. I cross the space and wrap my arms around his waist, laying my head on his broad chest. "So, friends?"

"Friends," he says, laying his cheek on top of my head.

I open my eyes, looking directly at Lexington.

Well, this is incredibly awkward.

"But I thought about what you said," Kai says, letting me go. "About taking the cure."

"And?" I ask him hopefully as I step away.

"I will take it, someday, hopefully soon." Kai looks over at Lexington, and slowly, I see something changing in his expression. The melting away of the view of an enemy. "But I know something has been going on. The city, it's not as safe as it used to be. I want to help."

I feel my entire body light up. "Kai, that sounds amazing."

"Aleah might take a bit to warm up to the idea of a Bitten helping her," Lexington says. "But we need all the help we can get."

"She'll have to accept it," I say, nodding my head. The confusion on Kai's face leads me to realize he has no idea what we're talking about.

A quick explanation of our plan, that we're essentially starting a new House to get everything back under control, and that Aleah and Duncan are in charge, brings him back up to speed.

"The ultimate plan is to turn whoever is willing over to Charles," I say. "They need to rebuild their House."

"Obviously you won't be joining the House when that time comes," Lexington says. I nod. Kai is a Bitten, and unless the Bitten have a Debt to one of the Born, they have no connections to the Houses. And that's illegal now. "But as you said, the plan is to eventually take the cure."

Kai nods his head, and I can see the wheels spinning in his head. "This could work," he says, a small smile on his lips. "I'll do it. I'll help this woman keep things under control."

I look over at Lexington, a full on smile spreading on my face. He returns it, and steps forward, his hand extended to Kai.

"Then welcome to the House of Martials."

chapter
SIXTEEN

"HOUSE OF MARTIALS, HUH?" I ask as Lexington drives us back from Cambridge.

"Sounds cool, doesn't it?" he says with a smile as we cross the bridge and make our way back into Boston. We just finished dropping Kai off, who took a bag of his things so he can stay for a few days and get acquainted with the operation Aleah has set up with Duncan and Robert.

Lexington was right, she wasn't thrilled about the idea of a Bitten joining her in the cause. There were a lot of nasty looks and curse words involved. But even she realizes how big of a region she has to work with, and just how difficult it is going to be to accomplish everything with just a few bodies.

"It makes sense I guess," I say as I look out the window at the dark night. "We are going above Charles' head and taking matters into our own hands."

"Feels kind of cool to be a revolutionary," Lexington says with a smile.

"It would feel cooler if innocent people weren't being caught in the crossfire," I counter. "But I guess. It's kind of weird not being on the sidelines."

Lexington makes a right turn and heads into my neighborhood. He rolls down the road and parks in front of the house.

"It's really nice to see you smile again," he says as we climb out and trudge through the snow. I unlock the front door and we step in, making our way up to my apartment. I open the door and we both take our boots and coats off. "You got kind of down for a little bit there."

I shrug, heading into the kitchen. I fill the kettle with water and set it on the stove. "I guess I didn't realize how hard it was, knowing the only friend I've had here in town was angry with me."

"Feelings sure do complicate things, don't they?" Lexington opens the fridge and pulls out a blood bag. Settling at the island, he pops it open and takes a long pull.

"I guess," I say, pulling out the can of powdered cocoa. I grab a mug from another cupboard. "I just…" I look down into it, unsure of how to say what's on my mind without embarrassing myself. "I've never had a serious relationship before. I barely know what it's like to have friends. So when things got complicated, I just didn't really know how to feel."

"I don't know that anyone does," Lexington says, leaning his forearms on the counter. "Heck, I'm over one hundred and sixty years old, and feelings still get me all twisted up."

Steam whistles through the kettle and I pour the water into the mug and mix in the cocoa. Pouring in a little cinnamon and milk, I go to sit beside Lexington at the counter. "You've lived a long time. I'm sure you've had some pretty significant relationships in your life."

Lexington shrugs. "Not as many as you might think. Being limited to only going outside in the dark can put a damper on your dating life. But I've had a few girlfriends over the many, many years," he says, looking down at the countertop. "Even asked a girl to marry me once, back in the thirties."

"What happened?" I ask, watching his face. He's always so casual and easy. But there's a hint of pain and struggle creeping onto it.

"She had a hard time really understanding what I was," he says. "I don't know that she really ever grasped just how long I'd lived. How strong the cravings could get." He twirls the half-drunk blood bag between his hands, staring at the red liquid inside of it. "I didn't have my thirst very under control back then. I mean, I was pretty good most of the time. I always tried to push myself, see how long I could go between feedings."

He rubs a hand down his face, looking tired suddenly.

"And occasionally I'd snap." He sinks his fangs into the bag, draining the rest of the blood from it. A small drop leaks out onto his lips. "She witnessed it once, about a week before I proposed. The man was fine, didn't even remember what happened afterwards because he was drunk at the time. Anita said she forgave me, that she could get over it."

"But she really couldn't," I fill in. The weight in his expression tells me I'm right.

He nods. "When I asked her to marry me, her eyes just filled with tears. She shook her head and just said 'I can't'. She said goodbye to me there on the docks in Maine."

I rest my hand on his back, rubbing in a small circle. "I'm so sorry," I say quietly. "That must have been so hard."

He shrugs. "Good thing I had eternity to get over it, right?" he forces a chuckle. But I really do feel his mood lift. His moods are like a physical thing, touching everyone around him, saturating into everyone else. "It proved good motivation to change my ways. I've been on a regular feeding schedule now for over ninety years, and no snapping incidents since."

I smile at that. "I will say, I've never once felt unsafe with you around."

A smile splits his face, full and bright. "Well, I'm glad to hear that. But Aleah wasn't lying. You do smell like dessert. All the time."

I feel my face flush and my eyes drop away from his as I can't fight the small smile. "Sorry to put you through so much torture."

Lexington doesn't say anything for a long moment and I finally look back at him. He studies me, taking in every one of my features. Long. Slow. "Not a moment here has been torture, I can assure you of that."

I look back and forth between his blue eyes, feeling the weight sinking into this moment. There's something growing in my chest, something soft but heavy. The breath stills in my chest.

Finally, Lexington cracks a smile on one side of his mouth.

"It's late," he says. He leans back, breaking the moment. I sit back, somewhat startled to be back in reality. "We've got to open the shop in the morning. You should get some sleep."

"Yeah," I say, blinking fast, clearing the fog from my head. I stand

and set my mug in the sink. But I can feel Lexington's eyes on me. I glance over my shoulder, and our eyes lock.

Something flutters in my stomach.

I cross to the front door, locking it. He follows me up the stairs.

"Goodnight," I say, looking back before I walk into my room.

"Sleep well," he says with this look on his face that I can't fully explain.

I close the door, leaning against it for just a moment to try to calm my racing heart.

It's bad, embarrassing, because I know without a doubt that he can hear it.

I push away from the door and go to my closet to change into pajamas. When I walk back into my bedroom, my phone dings from the nightstand. A text from a blocked number waits for me there.

Need an update in the morning. Hope I didn't wake you.

Ian.

He texts every so often, always from a different number, each a new burner phone so it can't be traced. He never calls though unless it's through the computer when Lexington can reroute the signals.

I look to the door, debating for a moment. I jump to my feet and pull the door open to go tell Lexington.

Light glows through the hallway, the sound of the shower coming from the second bathroom. I hesitate just outside my door, trying to listen for Lexington's location.

Movement through the crack in the door draws my attention to the bathroom. Lexington shifts into view. He sets something down on the counter, looking down for a few moments.

He then lifts his shirt, pulling it up and over his head, dropping it into the laundry basket in the corner.

A big scar lances from his right hip, zigzagging across his back, cutting over his spine before ending under his left shoulder blade. On his right shoulder blade is a tattoo, a list of three roman numerals.

The muscles of his back are defined and toned. With an immortal body he doesn't have to do much to maintain such a chiseled physique. Being the ultimate predator is in his Resurrected blood.

I feel my face flush, knowing I'm being creepy, standing here staring when he doesn't know I'm here. With one last glance, I step back into my bedroom, and close the door.

The ceiling stares back at me as I listen for the faint sound of the shower. I pull the covers up, crossing my hands over my chest.

I don't know if I trust myself in these things I'm starting to feel. I've never been in any kind of a relationship. I've only been on about a dozen dates in college, one since I moved to Boston. Do I really have any idea of what a relationship looks like? Of the things I'm supposed to be feeling for another person?

Lying to myself seems impossible though. There's something building in my chest, growing in my stomach, setting into my heart.

There's chemistry between Lexington and me. The comfortable ease I feel with him that I've never had with anyone else. The way we always seem to finish each other's sentences. The way he sticks up for me when I clam up and can't find the words. The fact that *no one* else has ever been able to get me to smile like he does.

I let out a slow breath between my lips, trying to push back these thoughts. I need sleep.

But as I roll over onto my side, all I can focus on is the sound of the water shutting off. The footsteps as they walk down the hall to the door across from mine.

The sound of that door shutting.

And the wish I have in my chest that there were no doors at all.

SEVENTEEN

THE NEXT DAY IS ONE of the most agonizing and long of my life. I consider myself to be more aware than most, having lived the life I have, knowing what I know. But the way I am hyperaware of *everything* Lexington does the next day is over the top.

Every movement he makes in the shop. The speed of his breathing. The amount of space between his body and mine. It's driving me insane.

It's making my chest hurt.

It's hard to breathe.

"Are you okay?" he finally asks around noon. He looks over at me with those blue eyes of his, his eyebrows slightly raised, a look of curiosity and concern on his face.

"Yeah," I say, looking away quickly before he can see the torment I'm feeling. "I just…I'm hungry I guess. Maybe you could run and get us some lunch?"

This brings a smile to his face. He's always saying I need to eat more regularly, and I knew it was one of the few things that would make him jump to leave. "Yeah," he says enthusiastically. "What are you in the mood for?"

I shrug. "Surprise me."

Somehow I also knew it would widen that brilliant smile. And I'm not wrong.

"K, I'll be back in a little bit." He winks at me as he walks out.

I watch him go through the windows until he's finally out of sight. I collapse back into my chair, feeling exhausted.

I wish I had someone to turn to for advice right now. Another female figure. Someone who could tell me how to deal with these overwhelming desires. How to proceed.

The only one I have though is Alivia. But I'm not supposed to communicate with her right now. And honestly I don't know that I want advice from her. She and my brother may be happy now, but they went through a million ugly words and months of fighting and turning to other people for comfort to get there.

I can't say that what's going on between Lexington and I looks anything like what Ian and Liv went through.

I think I'm grateful for that.

The bell above the door rings, and an older woman steps inside.

"Welcome to Oleander Apothecary," I say, flashing her what I hope is a warm smile. "What can I help you with today?"

She looks around the shop nervously, her eyes studying the different labels, the old shelves. She fidgets with the purse she carries.

"I hope I'm in the right place," she says. She turns in a little circle before continuing her walk to the counter. When she finally reaches it, she looks at me straight for the first time. "I'm a little unsure. You look far too young to be the one I heard about."

Once upon a time I might have gotten offended by her comment. But it's one that comes frequently. "I have a feeling I am in fact who you're looking for, actually."

She looks me up and down, studying me hard. I look her over similarly.

Her straight gray hair is cropped short, her skin wrinkled but tanned. She's thin, but not frail. There's something still very solid and lively about her.

"I heard you have products to ward off…night-loving problems," she says quietly, looking over her shoulder as if to make sure we are alone.

I straighten, my blood pressure spiking.

I get all kinds of strange requests here. But never anyone asking for things to ward off vampires.

"Where did you hear that?" I ask as the alarm bells start going off in my brain.

I don't sell my toxins.

Never have.

The only ones who know about them are my family, the House of Conrath, Kai, and King Cyrus.

"A rather unpleasant woman who took out my very suspicious neighbor," the woman says, looking around. "Young. Wore these wretched boots."

Aleah.

"I'm sorry," I say, anger raising my pulse all the more. "I can't say I know what you're talking about."

"You are Elle Ward, aren't you?" she asks, narrowing her eyes at me.

I nearly jump out of my skin, hearing my real name. My heart just about explodes and pin prickles break out onto my palms. My breath hitches. I swallow once, but to my credit, I've always had a good poker face. "Can't say I've ever heard of her. My name is Penny Jones."

The woman stares at me hard, confusion starting to settle into her expression. "I thought for sure…"

"I have an immobilizing spray," I cut her off, stepping out from behind the counter, pulling the stake out of my back pocket a bit, exposing the tip. "It's a bit like pepper spray, but ten times stronger."

I grab a bottle of it off the shelf and turn. The woman's eyes rise from the stake, to my eyes. She's trying to arrange her own poker face, but she's not as good.

"Yes," she says, pasting on a pleasant smile. "I think that will help."

I pleasantly smile at her and walk back to the register. "That'll be nineteen-seventy-five."

She pays cash and I put it in a bag for her. As she walks out, she looks back at me, narrowing her eyes in uncertainty once more.

The second she's gone, I duck into the lab and arm myself with stakes and toxins. I even slip a handgun into the waistband of my jeans.

I stand stiff behind the counter while I wait for Lexington to return, biting my thumbnail down to the quick. It feels like an eternity, and—how long could it possibly take for him to run down the street and get lunch?

When he finally rounds into view of the window, I step forward around the counter, catching my hip in my haste.

"What's wrong?" he immediately asks when he sees my face.

"There was this woman here just a few minutes ago," I say quietly as he sets the food on the counter. He stands close to me as I explain, looking around, checking to be sure we're alone.

"That doesn't seem right," he says. "I mean, it wouldn't be impossible for Aleah to figure your name out, but I don't think she'd tell anyone. She's a spitfire, but I don't think she'd turn against us like that."

"Lexington," I say and his eyes finally come back to mine. "What if she just made it all up? What if she works for Charles Allaway?"

It clicks in his head. "She could have been a spy," he breathes. "It's entirely possible she saw Aleah out doing her job. She could have followed us at any point from the House of Martials."

His breathing picks up speed, his nostrils flaring slightly. He stands on the balls of his feet, ready to spring into action at any moment.

He's two seconds away from something forceful, I can feel it as a tangible thing.

I reach up, placing my hands on either side of his face, forcing his eyes back to mine, even as my nerve endings explode at the physical contact. Everything in him stills, intensity burning in his eyes as he stares back at me.

"I'm not going to run," I say firmly. The resolve in my stomach hardens. "I've been bossed around by my brother my entire life, having to bend to the will and circumstances of the Born and the Bitten for longer than I can remember."

Lexington brings his hands up to my wrists, hanging on to me as I ground myself.

"I will fight. I *can* fight," I say, holding his eyes. "I have Kai. I have Duncan. I think you're right, Aleah wouldn't rat me out like that. And I have *you*."

Lexington nods, the intensity building in his eyes. He takes half a step forward, bringing his body closer to mine.

"I'm not running," I repeat, forcing every ounce of determination I can into my eyes.

He studies me, a look of awe in his eyes. "Fearless," he breathes.

And the next moment, he disappears. The bell on the door dinging loudly with the force he swings the door open with.

I'm slightly breathless. I blink fast, looking around the space, but he's disappeared.

I walk to the window, looking out to the busy street. There's no sign of him.

The speed of a vampire, especially a Born, is an incredible thing. But there are over seven hundred thousand people in this city.

Five minutes rolls by. Then ten. And Lexington doesn't immediately return.

I walk into the lab and pop open a cabinet. Inside is a shelf of stakes. Another with vials and needles. Another holds three dart guns. Another holds a portable solar light.

And the last holds incredibly thin glass orbs. A red liquid fills them.

Acid. Something I designed six years ago, just before I moved into the Conrath Estate, created specifically to burn the skin of a vampire.

I pull my jacket on, stocking up on even more weapons.

I may not be a hunter like Ian was before he Resurrected. I might not have training in martial arts, and I may not spend hours at the gym building physical muscle. But I am not helpless.

A sister for a sister.

But Charles isn't one to do his own dirty work. If he's really going to come after me, he'll send one of his few remaining followers.

The woman who came into the shop walked in during the brightness of day without any trouble. She's not a vampire, Born or Bitten.

If she was sent here on his behalf, he's using human spies.

It makes sense. In the past, the Born often used the Bitten to do their dirty work. But Charles hates the Bitten because of what they did to his sister, and he well knows it's illegal to create them now. He's limited on House members to do his bidding. But the one thing he does still have is money. And humans, if they need it badly enough, will do anything for money.

It's an hour before Lexington returns. His hair is wild, windblown. He's been running at vampire speed the entire time.

He shakes his head, anger rising in his eyes. "I didn't find her," he says. "The scent died off just down the road. Too many bodies to keep the trail."

I nod, going back to the window, crossing my arms over my chest.

"We're going to have to be more careful from now on."

Lexington walks up to stand beside me. He places a hand on my shoulder, his arm wrapping around me. "Get ready to have me glued to your side from now on."

I bite my lower lip, nodding.

This is about to get very interesting.

chapter EIGHTEEN

"A ND WHAT ABOUT THIS ONE?" Lexington asks.

I look up from where I harvest the very last of the wormwood, with its fuzzy leaves, beginning to crystalize in the winter air.

"White snakeroot," I say, looking back at what I'm doing. I clip the plant at the ground, clearing it to grow back next spring. "It normally has these tiny white flowers."

"And just how toxic is it?" Lexington asks, backing away from it half a step.

"Toxic enough you can be killed by drinking the milk from a cow who grazed on the plant. It's actually called 'milk poisoning.'"

"For real?" he asks, his eyebrows raising.

A little chuckle comes from my lips. "For real. It's how Abraham Lincoln's mother died."

"You scare me, poison sorceress," he says with a crooked smile.

"More than just a little."

I finish up, stuffing the last of the wormwood into the wooden crate. Dusting the dirt off my gloves, I nod my head back toward the stairs.

"I bet you know about seven different ways to kill me right now," he says as he follows me down into the laundry room. "Don't you?"

"More like nine," I say casually as I set the crate on a shelf where I will leave it to dry over the weekend.

He laughs, shaking his head at me as he takes his boots off and hangs his coat up. I hang mine, blowing hot air into my even more frozen than normal hands. I walk down the stairs into the living room, heading to the fireplace, when the boxes that occupy the space stop me.

I'd almost forgotten.

"Are you ready to do this?" Lexington asks, rubbing his hands together. I look back at him to see a ridiculous smile growing on his face.

"You realize how ludicrous you look right now?" I tease him.

"It's Christmas, baby," he says exuberantly. "'Tis the season for feeling jolly."

I laugh, shaking my head and turn back to the boxes.

"You're a vampire," I say as he cuts open the first box. "Doesn't celebrating Christmas feel a little … sacrilegious?"

"What are you talking about?" he demands as he pulls the artificial tree from the box. With invisibly fast hands, he has the tree pieces stacked and the branches fluffed out in no time at all, positioning it right in front of the window. "Christmas is for everyone. That's like, the one complaint I had about Liv's House. None of them cared that much about the holidays."

"And apparently you do," I say, remembering the huge shopping spree he dragged me along for last night.

"Yes, I do," he says, raising an eyebrow at me. With a smile, he plugs the lights in, colorful dots lighting up the room. "Now get over here and help me put this crap up."

I laugh, shaking my head at him. Lexington's enthusiasm isn't something I can deny. I stoop and pick up a bag of tinsel. Together, we wind it around the tree.

"You realize you're going to have to let me out alone sometime in the next three days so I can get you a present, right?" I ask as we start hanging the ornaments on the tree.

"You mean you've waited this long to get me something?" he teases, a look of mock hurt on his face.

"Hey," I say in defense. "You're literally with me every moment I'm not using the restroom or showering, and have been for the last how long now? Cut me some slack."

"Getting sick of me yet?" he asks, looking over and giving me a wink. But there's something genuine there that tells me he really is concerned about it.

The answer of no screams in my chest, and I feel my face flush slightly. I look away, paying attention to the little bells I hang from the branches. "No, not yet."

I can feel his eyes on me, watching far too closely.

I know there is something here, something building and growing, and it's becoming quite apparent that it isn't one-sided.

But I've never done this before. I don't know how to make the first move, don't have the words to initiate something.

And I think there's something holding him back too. Because the way my heart is racing from the way he's staring at me, and the way I know he can hear it, he's feeling this too. But he's not making a move either.

It's killing me.

"Tell me what you were doing in the sixties," I suddenly say as I move around the tree, trying to put a little distance between us so my body can cool down.

"The sixties," he says with a smile, turning his eyes back to the task at hand. "Oh man, you wouldn't have liked me in the sixties."

"Why is that?"

He chuckles, shaking his head at himself. "You know the phrase 'sex, drugs, rock and roll' came from that time period, right?"

I feel my expression fall. A cold stone sinks in my stomach.

"Well, maybe not the sex part," he says, oblivious to the grief it immediately brought me. "I mean, it's a little...dangerous, getting that close to someone if they aren't a Born as well. But the rock and roll, and the experimentation..."

My brows furrow. "That doesn't really sound like you."

He bends, grabbing another box of ornaments. "Well, I was feeling pretty lonely during that decade. My family was long, long gone. The few friends I had were moving on to other Houses, most back to Europe. Another was killed in some feud. Suddenly it was kind of just me and I guess it just ate me up for a while."

"That's terrible," I say, looking around the tree at him. He meets my eyes, a crooked smile coming to his lips.

"It was," he continues. He hangs a little reindeer toward the top of the tree, right next to a squirrel wearing a scarf.

He picked everything out. And I'm pretty sure we got the most random, eclectic assortment of tree decorations ever. It certainly isn't cohesive or pretty.

But it's quirky. Just like Lexington.

"The nightlife was the only option for me," he says. "I ended up in Philadelphia for about three years. Plenty of people to feed on. Lots of clubs. And so, so many new drugs to try to distract myself from the dead feeling inside."

I curse internally. It just keeps getting worse and worse, but he's saying it so casually and unaffectedly.

"Heroin was the best one," he says as he reaches up, setting the star at the top of the tree. "But man I had to shoot a lot of it to feel anything. I spent a fortune on the stuff."

"K," I say with a snap. "I get you did lots of drugs. How about moving on to something else."

He chuckles. "Sorry," he says. "It's so far in the past now I kind of forget the reality of it all was kind of a big deal. Let's see… Oh, the music. Rock and roll." A smile pulls back on his lips. "How do you like Jimi Hendrix?"

"Um," I say, pursing my lips together. "I mean, I know he's a legend, but…"

"I sometimes forget how young you still are," he laughs, his eyes twinkling as he looks back at me.

"Hey," I say, feeling irritation bristle in my chest. "I'm twenty-three now. My birthday was just last week. You dragged me out for cake, remember?"

He winks at me, something that says *you're still a baby*, but considering all else that's going on between us, he's not going to voice it out loud.

"I saw him live four times in two years," Lexington says as he begins setting up the random decorations throughout the room. On the coffee table, the bookshelf. In the window ledge. "Even went and bought myself a guitar because I was inspired by the man."

"You play?" I ask. My task finished, I sink onto the couch as he flips the lights off, casting us in the colorful glow of the tree.

"Yeah," he chuckles as he stands there, his hands in his pockets while he studies the tree. "Been forever though. Since I never got to go back to the House of Allaway for my stuff, my guitar and everything is probably still sitting in my old room. Man, I miss that thing."

I keep looking at him, standing there, staring at the tree. "How are you always so…easy, Lexington?" I ask quietly. "You've…you've lived through so much. Seen some terrible things. Been betrayed. Lost your family. How do you do it?"

He lets out a big breath, his shoulders sagging down. But he doesn't look away from the tree. "You can let your past define your life, let it constantly remind you every day of your failures and losses. But that's not how I want to be. I want a fresh start every day. A new beginning, over and over."

He looks over at me, the lights dancing in his eyes. "But I'm not always like this," he says. "I think you remember that."

I do. The Lexington I remember from five years ago was sarcastic and bitter and snarky.

"I'm not always like this," he says quietly, staring at me with intensity.

I sit there, in the twinkle of the tree, the night quiet, the air warm from the fireplace.

There are so many things I want to do in this moment. But they're all abstract concepts, floating just out of my reach.

But here, in the quiet night, *this* is enough.

Right now, it's just perfect.

chapter NINETEEN

"Y OU KNOW THAT I KNOW your name isn't Penny Jones, right?" Aleah says with annoyance as we head further downtown on the subway.

"I figured you did," I say, watching the lights flash by outside the windows. "I know you're a smart girl."

She doesn't say anything for a long moment. I've just complimented her and she didn't expect that. "Just saying."

Kai sits next to me, ear buds in, ignoring the rest of us. He's trying really hard to make this just friends thing work, but it's going to take some time.

I look up to where Duncan sits across from me. His eyes are fixed on the book he holds in front of his face, his eyes racing over the words faster than my human brain could actually process.

"Do you like to read?" I ask of Aleah as the subway makes a stop, letting more passengers off and even more of them on.

"Do I look like the type that likes to read?" she asks with a scoff.

"Sometimes people surprise you," I say. Duncan's eyes rise from the book for a moment, giving me a little knowing smile. He and his cousin couldn't be more different.

"Sometimes," Aleah says with a smug smile. "Like how Lexington is obviously super into you, yet somehow you two are managing to keep your hands off of each other?"

Anxiety jumps into my throat, and I sort of glance over at Kai. He doesn't react, and I hope and pray that he can't hear what was just said, but he is indeed a Bitten, whose hearing is better than mine.

I look over at Aleah, and she's giving me this look; very pleased with herself that she's gotten under my skin and is making me uncomfortable. As Duncan said, it's kind of her thing.

"I don't think it's really any of your business," I say, tucking a lock of hair behind my ear and looking away from her.

"You don't need to defend yourself," Duncan says, turning the page. Yet he never looks away from the book. "She just wants to rattle you, sticking up for yourself will just aggravate the game."

"Of course the girl should stick up for herself," Aleah says, staring at me through those kohl-lined eyes, a little smile pulling on her lips. "Who needs a knight in shining armor? This is the twenty-first century, is it not?"

"I—"

"Really, don't," Duncan says, looking up and glaring at his cousin. "She's just bitter. She's chased away every guy who's shown slight interest in the past decade with that attitude she wears as armor. Don't let her goad you into sparring for fun."

"Buzz kill," Aleah says, standing and walking to the other end of the subway car. She stares out the windows, watching the tunnels flash by.

"Her bark is worse than her bite," Duncan says, tucking a finger between the pages and closing the book. "And I have a feeling she's carried a little…thing, for Lexington for a few years now."

"Oh," I say, even as something sharp bites into my stomach.

"No," Duncan says, closing his eyes for a second and shaking his head. "Nothing like that. She just…she's never been one to not eye someone semi-decent looking. But she's the type to get bored quickly unless there's a challenge to it. She sees you looking at him and it just brings out the competitive nature in her."

"I don't think that makes me feel any better," I confess.

"Really, don't worry about it," Duncan says. "I think she's got her eye on this other guy anyway."

That brings a hint of relief to my chest, but not enough.

"Really, though," Duncan says, standing as the subway begins to slow, our stop approaching. "What's holding you and Lexington back? The chemistry there is pretty obvious."

The doors slide open and he and I step off, Aleah and Kai falling behind a little ways.

I so don't want to talk about this, not with Kai possibly hearing every word. And yet I do. I really need to talk to someone about this. And the situation with Kai may be awkward, but isn't honesty what I've been striving for with him in the last few months?

I shrug. "I'm scared, I guess. I've never done this before. And I'm worried we'll screw something up, and then we'll be stuck with each other, hating one another."

"But right now aren't you just miserable?" Duncan asks as we walk up the stairs and out to the street. "Being so close to what you want, but not ever getting quite close enough?"

The pain in his voice pulls my gaze to his face. There's real life experience there that brings out the truth to his words. "What about you, Duncan? Is there anyone special in your life?"

He shrugs, pushing his hands down into his pockets, pulling his sunglasses over his eyes in the dim evening light, even though he was given his first set of contacts a week ago. Everyone in the House of Martials has earned them. "It's complicated."

I'm not one to pry and he doesn't seem eager to share any more information.

The four of us make our way down the crowded road and head into the first store. We take our time, everyone fighting the crowds to get our Christmas shopping done. Kai gets some things for his mom and his sisters. Duncan grabs something for Aleah when she's across the store. I get both of them small gifts and agonize over what to get Kai. Something that can strike the balance of our new relationship.

Finally, after we've gotten dinner and the hour rolls toward seven, I pull out my phone, double-checking the address of our last stop on the store's website. I nod my chin toward the shop on the corner.

We step in, the smell of wood and steel and paper thick in the air. I instantly feel out of place, not knowing a thing about guitars other than the research I did on the computer last night.

"Are you Ingrid?" I ask, stepping up to the counter and getting the attention of the woman.

"You must be Penny," she says with a smile. "Give me just a minute and I'll go get it from the back."

Aleah wanders around the shop, plucking random guitar strings. Duncan stands beside me, his nose still glued in the book. A couple talks to another salesman on the other side of the store.

I glance over at Kai, but he won't meet my eyes. He just nods his head to his music.

A minute later, Ingrid walks back out, a guitar case in hand. She sets it on the counter, opening the lid.

"She's a classic," Ingrid says, nodding with a smile. "Someone sure is getting spoiled for Christmas."

She rings me up and I hand the cash over, waiting for my change.

"See, you don't fork out that kind of money, and put that kind of thought into a present for someone you don't really, really want to be with," Duncan says without looking up.

I blush, not looking at him. But from the back of the store, I hear Aleah breathe, "Whipped."

We make a two more stops, and I grab a few more items. Aleah picks up some things, Duncan buys three more books and a cup of coffee. Just after ten, we head back for the subway when Aleah's phone rings.

"Yeah, Robert?" she says as she answers it. The four of us stop, turning to watch her expression as she listens.

"What?" Aleah snaps into her phone. Her eyes dart around, listening to the voice on the other end. "How long does it take to get to Providence from here?" she asks me.

"About an hour," I say. "As long as there isn't traffic. We should be okay this time of night."

She glances toward the subway entrance, a block from where we've stopped on the sidewalk. "I don't have time to wait. Yeah, I know," she growls into the phone. She sets off down the road at a quick pace, in the opposite direction of the subway station. "Meet us there in an hour."

She hangs up, sliding the phone into her back pocket. She stops beside an older SUV.

"What are you doing?" I ask as I watch her walk around to the driver's door. She fiddles with it, and a second later, she pulls the door open.

"She's steeling this car," Duncan says, pulling open the passenger door when Aleah leans across the consul and pushes it open. "Get in."

"Are you kidding me?" Kai says, the first word he's spoken since we set out on what was supposed to be an innocent shopping trip.

"What?" I breathe, taking one step back. "We're stealing it?" I look side to side, but no one is around.

"Robert has been patrolling Rhode Island the past two days," Aleah says impatiently. "He just got a hit, followed them, and found a whole mess of Bitten. We're making a pit stop at your shop."

My heart jumps into my throat, and suddenly taking this car that doesn't belong to us doesn't feel like such a big deal.

I throw the guitar and my other purchases into the trunk and duck into the back seat with Kai.

Fifteen minutes later, we stop in front of Oleander Apothecary. With Duncan and Kai at my side, we dart inside.

First, I head straight to the basement. "How many doses?" I ask as I unlock the hidden door, digging through vials.

"Bring it all just in case," Duncan says, grabbing the other supplies I point at. Kai grabs a cooler from upstairs, and helps me carefully load everything in.

"You want me to just grab all the toxins?" Kai asks as he takes the cooler and we dart back upstairs.

"Let's get it all," I say as we slip into the lab and I unlock the cabinet that holds everything deadly and important.

"You know how to use all this stuff?" Duncan asks as he holds a bag open for me. The look on his face is more than just a little shocked.

"I'm the one who invented it all, so yes," I say, watching as Kai slips the last of the acid orbs into the bag. I snatch the UV flashlight off the shelf for good measure. I grab the cooler, taking one last look around to be sure I have everything. Shutting off the lights, the three of us head back outside, and I lock the door behind us.

"Supplies like that," Aleah says, shaking her head as we pull away from the curb back onto the road. "You come from hunter blood. I'm going to have to start watching my back."

"Maybe just watch what you say from now on," I say breathlessly as

I'm thrown back in my seat as she hits the gas.

"Lexington's not picking up," Duncan says, hanging up. "It's going straight to voicemail. His phone must be dead."

He's out Christmas shopping as well, somewhere in this massive city.

"You can't go with us, El…uh, Penny," Kai says as I'm thrown against his side when Aleah takes a sharp turn. "If there are a lot of them—"

"We don't have time to drop her off and find a babysitter," Aleah says with a growl. "And we need as many bodies as we can get, and with everything she just brought out of that shop, I'm inclined to think she's somewhat capable."

I grab my phone, pulling up my text feed with Lexington. *Where are you?* I send.

But it doesn't say *delivered*.

I look out the window as we fly through the night. Racing into an unknown, dangerous situation. But as my heart pounds, the smile grows on my face.

How much my life has changed in the past few years. When I lived in the South I was constantly shuffled to the side, out of the line of action. Someone to lock away when things got dangerous.

Now here I am, in the center of the action.

I'm proud of those scars that line my arms.

I'm still alive when everyone thinks I shouldn't be.

I love my brother. But he's been holding me back.

Darkness blankets the world as we race from Boston to Providence. Out to the outskirts where Robert directs us. Out through fields. And finally, into a tiny town with only a few dozen houses.

"That must be it there," Aleah says, nodding her chin toward a seemingly abandoned warehouse. She pulls the car off the road behind some bushes. She turns in her seat, addressing Duncan and I. "Okay, here's the plan. Kai and I are going to find Robert, we're going to scope out the full span of this thing. You two wait here, watch for my signal. If it's a no go, I want you both to get out of here. If it looks like there's something we can do, you both better be ready to get your hands dirty."

Duncan and I nod, and Aleah climbs out, Kai on her tail, quietly shutting the doors behind them. We both watch as they dart across the road, nothing more than a blur. From behind an outbuilding, steps Robert.

His shaved head gleams in the moonlight, his beard masking much of his face. His dark skin, the leather jacket, and black pants make him nearly invisible in the night.

"You getting a weird vibe from this place?" Duncan asks as he opens his door.

"I think weird is the only vibe I'm used to these days," I say quietly as I pull my supplies into the seat and start going through them.

"How does all this stuff work?" he asks as I start handing him things.

"The toxins immobilize a vampire, Born or Bitten, instantly," I say, handing him two vials and fishing around for another dart. "These will burn the skin, slowing them down significantly." I climb out of the car and place two orbs in his hand, which he slips into his pocket. "And if worse comes to worse, good old fashioned stakes."

I've just slapped one down in his hand, when Duncan suddenly looks over his shoulder. He whips around, eyes instantly red, fangs bared, but three figures rush at us, too late to react.

A man slams into me, knocking me hard against my back into the car. My head snaps back, the wind expelling from my lungs. Yellow eyes burn into mine as he howls in my face, yanking the stakes in my hand out of my grasp, launching them into the night.

He whips me around, throwing me to the ground, shoving my cheek into the dirt.

Duncan roars in fury as he fights off two others, and suddenly two more run out from the trees surrounding us.

"Behind you!" I scream.

Duncan grabs the woman by the throat, his fingers disappearing into her flesh and a trail of blood leaking down her neck. He spins, launching her toward the other two, pieces of her esophagus still in his hand.

He whips around, stake in hand to put down the other, but the man kicks his foot out, knocking Duncan flat to his back.

"Go find the other two!" the man on top of me yells, distracted for just a moment long enough.

I twist beneath him, bringing my necklace up to my lips, and puff. A needle launches up into his throat.

Instantly, he drops to the ground with a hiss, his body convulsing.

"Duncan!" I yell, just as the two he'd previously knocked to the ground launch through the air at him.

Bringing my dart gun to my lips, I fire off a shot, narrowly missing the man.

They both drop straight onto Duncan's chest, fangs bared, yellow eyes brilliant in the dark night.

I pull one of my orbs from my jacket pocket and launch it at the woman on top of him. It shatters against her cheek and she scrambles away, screaming in pain, holding her burning face.

The wind instantly knocks from my chest as someone plows into me from behind, sending the both of us to the ground. They yank my arms behind my back, quickly tying them tightly together.

"Got 'em!" someone yells across the road.

I'm yanked up to my feet, a strong hand holding me by the ropes around my wrists, and a hand fisted in my hair.

Duncan is jerked to his feet as well, chains looped around his wrists, a stake held firmly to his back.

"Aleah!" he yells, his eyes fixed on the form of the warehouse across the road.

My human eyes strain to see through the dark, the only light coming from the half moon and the stars.

But I see the form of Aleah being shoved in front of the doors, stumbling as someone yanks on her chains. A second later, Robert drops to his knees, not looking very conscious. And lastly Kai is pushed over, falling on his side in the dirt.

"Well, well," a voice calls, located up too high. As I'm marched forward, I search around for its source. And I see a figure walking along the roof of the warehouse, at the same time a huge door rolls back on the warehouse.

And a dozen yellow eyes glow from within its depths.

"I see some Born got a little jealous of our party," the voice cuts through the night again. As we get closer, I make out the figure of a man, his features slowly coming into view. But his yellow eyes are unmistakable. "Just couldn't stand to be left out of all the fun."

The man looks to be in his mid-forties. Well-kept hair is offset by a scruffy looking beard, peppered with silver. Crows feet spread out from his eyes, his entertained smile almost too wide for his face.

He wears jeans, and heavy looking boots. A denim jacket is buttoned up to his neck. From one hand, he swings a stick. The end of it has a chain hanging from it, and attached to that is some kind of orb, with stakes sticking out of it in every direction.

High school history lessons tickle the back of my brain to find the name of such a medieval weapon:

A flail.

"If you needed some company you should have found one of your prestigious Houses," he says, sounding very dangerous and angry. "You won't find much love here."

I look around, and slowly, the yellow eyes surround us. There has to be nearly twenty of them.

"I don't know what you think you're doing here," Aleah says, glaring up at the man on the roof. "But it's going to get you killed pretty quick these days."

The man laughs, a quick, one-huff thing. "And who's around to stop me?" He throws his hands out wide, as if displaying all the free run he's gained.

"Haven't you heard about the King's decree?" Duncan says, looking up, more bravery in his eyes than I expect to see.

"King?" the man says. "See, I've heard legend about some king. But it's a little hard to believe he's real when he's not around to slap me on the hand."

Heavy nostril breathing draws my attention to my left. Two Bitten slowly walk toward me, their eyes brilliant. Their nostrils flare and their fangs lengthen.

"Leave her alone!" Kai suddenly bellows, lunging toward me. Two other Bitten throw themselves on top of him, taking him back to the ground.

"So nice of you to bring a snack," the man on the roof says. "But let's save her for a little later, shall we boys?"

The two eying me instantly stop, though they continue to stare at me with hunger in their eyes.

"He's their sire," I say, staring back at them. "Their Debt is to him."

Aleah looks from the ones who stopped, to the man up on the roof. "What's your name?"

"Michael," he says loudly, as if he's very proud of the fact. "Michael Savage. And this is my band of brothers."

"Are they really brothers if they're just slaves?" Duncan pipes up.

A heavy fist meets him in his middle and he doubles over, nearly dropping to the ground but held up by the meaty man behind him.

The Born are better and stronger than the Bitten. But right now Aleah, Robert, Kai, and Duncan are outnumbered six to one.

"You tell your men to keep their damn hands off my cousin!" Aleah screams into the night.

"Let me guess, show some respect for the Born, right?" Michael says as he squats down on the edge of the roof, a look of entertainment in his eyes.

"Oh," Aleah says with a chuckle. "It wasn't like that before, but you're about to make it."

He hops down from the roof, landing on his feet with ease. He saunters over to her, his gait casual and easy. "It's been that way from the dawn of time, darlin'," he says as he crouches down, taking her chin in his hand, forcing her face up at him. "Though I am surprised to see you've got one of us running around with your kind."

Aleah's eyes flash red and she snaps her fangs at him.

"Oh ho!" he says, snatching his hand away. "This one is a feisty one! I like her style!"

"You have no idea what you've done here," Duncan says, rolling his head back up, standing straight. "The creation of any new Bitten is punishable by death now."

"You know, I have heard about this mysterious King," Michael says, turning away from Aleah. "That he lives somewhere over in Europe, far, far away. I also heard that this supposed decree was made six years ago. *Six years*, and here I am. Turned three years ago. No one but me killed my sire. I've made myself dozens of friends since, and no one has come after me."

"It's not the way it's supposed to be," I say. My voice cuts through the night like a knife, all eyes turning to me.

Michael turns, slowly walking forward. His eyes gleaming. Everything about him is a predator. "I assume you're talking about the Allaway fellow."

I don't say anything in return and he stops just two feet in front of me.

"Yeah, I've heard about him," Michael smiles. It's a crooked thing, bigger and wider on the left side than the right. And it's sickeningly charming. "Seems to me he's either lost his nerve, his power, or his interest. Either way, I'm having a lot of fun."

"And what do you think is going to happen when you expose your kind?" I ask, holding his gaze without faltering. "When the people realize they have a reason to fear the night, and they come out with their pitchforks and torches? When the billions of them turn against the thousands of you?"

He lets out an amused chuckle, his smile growing just slightly. "You surprise me, Mary Sue. A pretty, little young thing, running around with vampires, spittin' fire."

"Not everything is what it seems," I say without wavering.

Michael suddenly stands upright. "Nobody touches this one," he says as he looks out over the crowd. "I like her. I think I'll keep her for myself, her fate to be determined at a later time."

Laughter rings out through the crowd. I swear they all shift just a little tighter and closer. Kai swears in Samoan, his eyes glowing and brilliant as he tries to fight against the now four men who hold him down.

Oh, if only Ian were here.

Every one of them would be dead by now.

But I have to remind myself, as I look around at the faces of all these men. They don't have a choice in this. They're just doing whatever Michael Savage has told them to do.

"Bring them inside, boys!" he yells, waving his hand as he walks toward the small house that sits off to the right of the warehouse.

chapter
TWENTY

THE MAN BEHIND ME ROUGHLY yanks me to the side, walking in the direction of the house. The bodies mass around us, walking us five hostages to the front door. Up rickety steps we rise and through a squeaky door. The lot of us are herded into a smaller living room.

Michael sets his flail on top of the piano against one wall and takes a seat in a high backed chair, propping his feet up on the coffee table. I'm roughly shoved down onto a couch, tumbling over. I glare at the man who tossed me, but he just offers an amused smile.

Other Bitten force Kai, Duncan, Aleah, and Robert onto the same couch. We don't really fit, and we're all half sitting on one another. Each of them has a Bitten behind them, a stake held to their backs.

"Now, isn't this cozy?" Michael says with a smile as he looks around at the many bodies packed into the room. "Dixon, why don't you go get us all something to eat?"

A man in the corner nods his head and immediately heads out the door once more.

"Now, how about you explain what you're doing here, intruding on my land?" he says as he grabs a handful of nuts from a bowl on the table.

"There's been some problems—"

"Not you," Michael cuts Aleah off, giving her a harsh glare. "Her."

He nods his chin at me, chewing the nuts slowly, studying me carefully. He's testing me, seeing if I'm worth my weight.

But he doesn't know I'm far more versed in these politics than he is.

"All of your kind is causing a problem in this area," I say, raising my chin just slightly. To my surprise, the man who hauled me in here cuts the ropes around my wrists. Instead of rubbing them like I want to, I set them in my lap. "Born *and* Bitten. You know who Charles Allaway is, I'm guessing you know he's supposed to be in charge of keeping all of the vampires under control in his region."

"Something stuffy like that," Michael says with a smile, still chewing.

"He's weak right now, he doesn't have the power to keep everyone in check," I continue. I shift my hand just slightly, covering the pocket of my pants, slowly sliding out my compact dart gun. "So we're trying to do his job for him."

"As I understand it, Charles is theoretically some kind of Royal, a descendent of this supposed King." Michael drops his feet back to the floor, leaning forward, resting his elbows on his knees. "And the five of you are just going to undermine his authority?"

"There isn't much choice anymore," I say, holding his gaze. "If he doesn't do his job, the Born and the Bitten are going to get your kind exposed. The King will be forced to deal with things himself." I swallow once, sitting just a little straighter. "Trust me. You don't want him getting involved."

Michael studies me for a minute, searching my eyes as his expression grows serious. "You've met the man, haven't you?"

"Yes," I reply.

He nods, continuing to look at me. "I believe you. This King is the real deal, despite how unbelievable it all sounds."

"Then I hope you understand why you have to stop what you're doing?" I say evenly. "You're putting more than just a few people in danger."

The man named Dixon suddenly steps back into the room, shoving a teenage boy in front of him. The kid stumbles onto the floor, looking up at all the eyes that suddenly flash yellow.

The kid is human, apparently.

"Hold up just a minute," Michael calls loudly, holding his hand up when half of his Bitten step forward, their fangs lengthening. "From what we've just been told, doing what we've been doing is punishable by death."

Michael stands and looks around to those who have a Debt to him. They wait on him, on edge, ready to jump at the slightest command from him. "So when you drink, make sure you take it all."

It's all they need. Nearly every one of them leaps forward, sinking their fangs into the boy, just before he lets out a terrified scream.

I pull the blow gun from my pocket, placing it to my lips, and puffing, hitting the nearest man in the neck with a toxin, at the same time Duncan breaks free from his loosened chains and throws two of the orbs, screams instantly ripping into the air.

I fire off three more shots, each needle hitting its mark, at the same time Duncan whips around, staking the man behind him. Kai leaps up, swinging his left foot and connecting with the head of the man who held a stake to his back.

Aleah flips over the couch, hooking her chains around her own captor's neck, pulling tighter and tighter, until the chains disappear into his neck.

I turn my back before I can see her pop his head off.

A man charges at me, but not before I pull the cure from my inside pocket and fling it at him. He goes down with a scream, as does the next man who rushes at me.

Robert jumps, getting his hands in front of his body, and smashes the coffee table. He grabs the wooden shards, and flings two stakes, taking out the Bitten.

In just a few seconds, we've taken out half of Michael's Bitten.

"Take them down!" he bellows, scrambling for his flail.

Ten more Bitten rush toward us.

"It doesn't have to be like this," I hiss as the five of us back toward the wall. The three Born with me are stronger, faster than the Bitten, two of them, and Kai, are still chained, and we're still outnumbered. "Let's talk, and no more of them have to die, Michael."

"Seems to me you're still outnumbered," he growls as he swings his spiked ball back and forth. His muscles are tensed, ready to spring.

"Seems to me we took out half your men in less than ten seconds," Aleah taunts. "And half of those were taken down by our human."

Michael's eyes flash brighter as his eyes flick back to mine. A chuckle bubbles up from his lips, which quickly grows into a laugh.

But it's cut short, when one of his men lunges toward us. A fraction of a second later, Robert buries another table shard into his chest.

"Please stop!" I yell as my eyes widen in horror. Another innocent is dead, never to live again. "You need to stop or I will kill you myself! They don't all have to die!"

Michael's eyes widen, his jaw clenching. He takes one step forward, standing straight. He swings his bat back and forth. "You, a tiny human, are going to threaten me?"

I pull out a stake in one hand, holding my loaded dart gun in the other.

"You think you can kill me?"

"I know I can," I say, my gaze steeling.

Michael takes one more step forward, and I bring my blow dart up to my lips. I gather my breath, ready to blow at any second.

A laugh breaks from his chest, just one huff. But then it's followed by another. And soon he's absolutely losing it. Full-bellied, face toward the ceiling.

But I don't relax. I'm holding that breath in, prepared to fire toxins into his body.

"Holy *shit*, this has taken an interesting turn," he finally says, taking in a deep breath. "I have to say, I never expected this. To get absolutely schooled by a little blondie human."

A smile curls on one side of his face as his eyes fix on me once more. "I'm absolutely intrigued."

My brows furrow. My hand curls a little tighter around the stake in my left hand.

I just about loose my dart when he stretches his right hand forward.

"Whoever the hell you are, little girl," he says, cocking a smile. "Count me in on your team with whatever you've got planned."

No one moves for a second, no one says a word.

"Are … are you serious?" Aleah says, her tone absolutely disbelieving. "That's all it took? Penny kicking your ass?"

Michael looks over at Aleah, his face just as shocked. "If someone like her can kick my ass, she sure as hell has my interest. I've got some learning to do, apparently."

"Just like that?" Duncan questions, not convinced.

"Just like that," Michael says with a smile.

There's something about him that reminds me of Markov. Deadly. A wild cannon. A slave to his thirst. And absolutely mad.

"Prove it," I say, standing a little taller, only pulling my dart gun away from my lips slightly. "Tell all your men to line up against that wall." I nod my chin to the one by the front door.

Michael studies me for a moment longer. Suddenly he swings his bat over his shoulder, the spiked ball hanging dangerously in the air just above his back.

"You heard her, boys," he says loudly. He turns to them. "Line up."

Without hesitation, each and every one of them, the nine that
left, line up single file against the wall. Right behind the body of the no
dead boy they drained in just seconds.

"Watch him," I say to the four at my side. They all crouch just a little
deeper, their hands ready for action. Kai hisses at me under his breath,
begging me to be careful.

I slip my blow dart back into my pocket, though I keep the stake in
my left hand. Reaching inside my jacket, I produce a needle, full of the
amber tinted cure.

"You can't do this to them," I say, shaking my head. "Slaves aren't
friends. They aren't family."

"Worked fairly well the last three years," he says. "But you seem to
have a better way."

I don't know about that, but whatever the hell I'm doing, it seems to
be having a magical effect on Michael.

"You have to let them go," I say as I step over a body and stop in
front of the first man. I sink the needle into his shoulder, depressing the
plunger. Instantly, he hisses in pain, doubling over.

"What are you doing to him?" Michael demands, lunging forward
two steps.

Instantly, Kai is in his face, pressing a stake to his chest.

Oh how the tables have turned quickly.

"I'm freeing him," I say, moving on to the next Bitten, who stands in
line, his eyes wide and scared as he watches his fellow brother curl on
the floor in pain. I plunge the needle into the next arm. He collapses too.

"She cures them," Aleah says, the slightest hint of reverence in her voice.

"No shit," Michael says in shock as his eyes dart back to the two men on the floor, curling in pain. "Didn't know that was possible."

"It's not, so far as the rest of the world knows," Aleah says, giving him a deadly look.

Michael smiles again, chuckling in amusement. He shakes his head. "Don't know what you're taking about. I didn't see nothing." He winks at me, just as I depress the needle into the next man's arm.

One by one, I move down the line, injecting the cure into each and every one of them. Next I move on to the men on the floor that I shot with the toxin.

For a little bit, the room is deafening with their cries of pain. But slowly, each of them suddenly grows quiet, finally slipping into unconsciousness.

"They'll be out for twenty-four hours," I say, setting all the now empty vials on a table by the door. "I suggest you be very convincing when they wake up, to get them not to say anything about what's happened. All of it."

"I do consider myself to be a persuasive man," Michael says, studying the men who are now all sleeping.

"Please let them all go," I say, nodding to Kai, Duncan, Aleah, and Robert, who still have their hands chained together.

He laughs, shaking his head again, and steps forward.

"I don't trust you," Aleah says as she's un-cuffed. "Just so you know."

"Sounds like you're a smart woman," Michael says, winking at her as he undoes Robert, before moving on to Kai. "But I did say I'd help, and

I consider myself to be a man of my word."

"We're trying to build numbers," I jump in, taking the open opportunity to convince him that what we're doing is worthwhile.

Michael settles down into his chair once more, all casual and relaxed, like he isn't surrounded by bodies.

"The House of Allaway isn't doing its job, but that doesn't mean we have to let our region go to hell," Aleah says, standing in front of the couch with her arms folded over her chest. "We patrol the region, talking sense into those who will listen, putting down those who are just problems."

"You're the King's unknown mafia," Michael says with a smile. "I like it."

Each of us is staring at him with similar looks of disbelief. I'm wondering if he is completely insane. We've just ripped everything he's built out from under his feet, and he just seems to be enjoying the turn of events.

Aleah closes her eyes for a second, shaking her head. "Okay. Uh," she claps her hands in front of her. "What we need is members. Others to help us patrol. Take care of problems."

Michael looks over at me. "Was this your plan, blondie?"

Suddenly I realize just how much pressure Alivia was under the past few years. This is all about saying just the right thing at the right time, getting people to do what needs to be done.

It's up to me to convince this one man. She had an entire House to win over all on her own.

"Yes," I tell him.

"Oh, I'm in then," he says, tilting his head to one side, smiling that manic smile.

A quiet curse comes from the door.

"About time you showed up," Aleah says.

I turn, my heart picking up speed before my eyes even find his.

Lexington stares back at me, his knees bent, his hands curled into fists, looking ready for anything.

My heart races in my chest. My skin comes electric, static pulling every cell in me to life.

The way he's looking at me, something has changed in it.

"Get a room," Aleah growls. I tear my eyes away from Lexington, turning to see her roll her eyes.

Michael chuckles, entertained once more by this turn of events.

"How are we supposed to know if we can trust you?" Aleah asks, folding her arms over her chest.

"Because I know you need more than just my kind," Michael says, and a hint of bitterness creeps into his voice. "You need more Born, and I'm gonna' tell you where you can find two of 'em that I'm pretty sure will join you in a heartbeat."

The lot of us look at one another, still not believing the evolution this little trip has gone through.

From hostages, to room full of bodies, and a man pledging to help us grow the House of Martials.

"You'll take us to them right now," Aleah says, taking a step toward him. "And if they don't join us, I'll kill you."

"Oh, honey," Michael says, smiling at her. "You could try."

chapter
TWENTY
ONE

WE WALK OUTSIDE, ALEAH CARRYING a stake just two inches from Michael's back, but he carries his flail. "They live in Raynham, about halfway between here and Boston."

"Sounds good," Aleah says, shoving him forward. "Where's your vehicle? We need to get moving so you can get back here before tomorrow night when all your friends wake up."

The two of them head to a truck parked off to the side of the warehouse.

"I'll go with Lexington," I say when Duncan turns concerned eyes on me. And I can't help but give a side look to Kai.

He gives me this little thin-lipped look but nods. "It's okay, I'll go back with these guys." He takes a step back toward the stolen SUV, not looking back as he walks away.

Duncan gives me a knowing look, but doesn't say anything as he and Robert head to the vehicle.

I watch Lexington's face as I follow him back to his car. He opens the door for me, and I slide in, not liking the stiff line of his lips, the way his jaw is clenched. He climbs into the drivers seat and starts the engine.

"How'd you find us?" I ask, unsure of what kind of mood he's in. That's a first.

"Phones can do amazing things these days," he says as he pulls out onto the road behind Aleah and Michael. "I tracked you to about twenty feet of your location."

"Oh," I say, looking down at my hands. I realize then that there's a spray of blood across them and dirt smeared up to my wrists.

I reach up, feeling the dirt on my face as well from when the Bitten shoved me down.

"You okay?" he asks in a tight voice.

I look over at him, so wary of how to proceed. "I'm fine. They didn't hurt me."

He lets out a little short breath through his nostrils and gives a curt nod.

"Lexington, I—"

"I'm not mad at you," he says, holding a hand up. "We'll…we'll talk about this later."

I look at him again, my brows furrowing. I'm so confused right now. In the past month and a half that we've been with each other, he's never once been mad. And despite him saying he's not, he sure seems it.

Everything about his mood is rocked right now.

Instead of digging, I sit in my seat in silence, and turn to watch the pitch-black night pass by outside.

An hour later, we roll to a stop outside a singlewide trailer in the middle of nowhere. Michael and Aleah climb out, holding a hand up for the rest of us to stay where we are. The two of them walk inside after knocking and a woman opens the door.

The silence is so awkward as Lexington and I just sit in the dark car, waiting for a signal. I'm too aware of the stiffness of his shoulders. The way he keeps rubbing his left hand over his mouth. The way his right is curled into a fist, resting on his leg.

I'm dying to know what's on his mind.

But I think I'm too scared to find out.

Twenty minutes roll by. Duncan climbs out of the car, leaning against it, folding his arms over his chest.

"Can you hear what's going on?" I ask, not looking at Lexington.

"No," he says. His voice is tight. "They've got music playing, pretty loud. They don't want us hearing whatever they're talking about."

That makes me nervous, but Aleah did say she was going to use her own methods when it came to the cause.

Thirty minutes pass. I faintly see movement through the windows, but it's too dark for my eyes to pick up on much.

Finally, just short of an hour after we pulled up, the front door opens again. I see Aleah and Michael come out, barely able to pick their faces out. And next follows two more figures, each carrying a large bag over their shoulder.

They walk up to Lexington's car, features coming into view as they come closer.

Two women follow Aleah, both looking to be close to thirty.

"We're good," Aleah says, casting us a smug smile. "We'll head back to the House and then the two of you can be on your way to wherever it is you hide out."

Lexington just gives her a nod and watches as they walk away. One of the women goes to Michael's car, the other goes to Duncan's.

"That puts us up to six members, if we count you, eight if we count Kai and Michael," I say as we pull back on to the road. "It's a start."

"It's a start," he says, staring straight ahead and out the window.

THIRTY MINUTES LATER WE ROLL into Cambridge and stop in front of the House. Lexington and I walk inside and the two women introduce themselves. There's Julie, she's actually very friendly and bubbly, with wavy red hair and a ton of freckles that make for a beautiful woman. And then Eva, who reminds me a lot of Aleah, with her dark, somewhat disheveled clothes, and long dark hair that looks like she doesn't care too much how it looks. She doesn't say much, just wanders around the house, analyzing everything.

We aren't given an explanation as to why they've decided to join us. And I'm honestly too drained and too physically and emotionally tired to get into it all.

"I've got this," Aleah says as she and Duncan walk us back to the front door. Kai already took off without saying much. "I'll get them filled in, figure stuff out. Get her home." Aleah studies me, and to my surprise, a tiny smile crooks on her face. "But watch yourself, there's more to this one than meets the eye."

It's a white flag, a compliment of truce.

I've earned her respect today, and I have a feeling it's going to change a lot between us.

"Thanks," Lexington says, and waves as we walk out the door.

Once more, he holds the door to the car open for me, but the awkwardness grows as he climbs in. Without a word, we make our way through the streets. We cross the bridge.

Just five blocks from home, snow begins falling from the sky.

We park in front of the house and climb out. I look up as we walk up to the front door, seeing the fat flakes drift through the dark night.

I close my eyes, my feet stopping. Just standing there for a moment.

My life is never, ever going to be normal. No matter how far away I live from Silent Bend. No matter how hard I try to stay out of the affairs of the vampires.

I'm not one of them. I never will be.

But I'm ever a part of their world.

"Elle?"

I open my eyes and find Lexington watching me from the front door. Taking a deep breath and letting it out, I finish the trip.

Shrugging my coat off and hanging it in the closet, I flip the gas fireplace on. And try as hard as I can to look anywhere *but* at him, my eyes lock on him as he too takes his coat off.

He stands there, in jeans and boots and a dark blue v-neck t-shirt, his hands on his hips, his lips thin and his expression grim. He stares at the floor.

"You remember that time, before the Battle of the Bitten," he says, his voice rough. "When everything was so crazy and they had us surrounded. And Markov was pretty mangled and got his leg broken and he was so roughed up?"

I nod, my throat thick.

"Yeah," I say.

"And you remember the way his eyes flashed red and he looked at you," Lexington says, shaking his head.

"He wanted my blood," I say.

"And I hauled you out of there and we sat in your room for the rest of the night." He shifts from one foot to the other, rubbing a hand over the back of his neck. "I just kept waiting for him to haul up those stairs and bust down your door. I half thought I was going to have to kill him that night so he wouldn't drain you."

My brows furrow. I remember the night well, but I have no idea why he's bringing this up now.

"We didn't say much that night, but I think it kind of made an impact," he says, sniffing, and he still won't look at me. He paces a few steps back and forth. "See, it was the first time I really made a choice to help someone in Liv's house. Not just because Cyrus told me I needed to be loyal or he'd kill me. It didn't have to be me that stood guard over you, could have been Cameron or Christian or Lillian."

My heart starts beating faster. I want him to hurry and get to the point, because I'm getting more confused by the minute.

"And that changed something for me, made me realize that I didn't just have to *bear* everything after the trade," he continues. "I could choose to make this new situation be a good thing." He shakes his head back and forth. "But that night, I think my image, my impression of you locked in on that one act. The girl I chose to help, the fragile one that needed *my* help and I chose to take it."

He turns his back to me, bracing his hands on the wall, sagging his head between his arms. "When Ian asked me to come here and keep an eye on you, I was back at that night, choosing to help that same fragile girl. I'm just one in a House that is pushing thirty. And *I* was needed."

He brings his head up and he shakes it. His breathing is deep, rough.

"But after the past few weeks, after tonight..." He's suddenly very still, standing with his back to me. I want to see his face, to read him. "Elle. You don't need me. You don't need anyone. Your brother may think you're helpless, but he's never really seen the true Elle Ward."

Something swells in my chest at his words.

Truth.

My entire life everyone has underestimated me. Tried to protect and shelter me.

I always knew I could take care of myself. But I let them think what they needed to about me.

But here, Lexington has just stripped it all away.

"I know one hundred percent you'll be just fine without me here, Elle," he says as he lets his hands fall away from the wall. His arms sag at his side, his shoulders slumped.

A swarm of garden butterflies unleash in my stomach.

"But I want you here."

Lexington is very still for a moment. Frozen by my words.

Slowly, he stands up straight. Slowly he turns to look at me as my own truth finally breaks free from my lips.

His eyes connect with mine, so very bright, dancing in the light of the Christmas tree.

"You're right," I say, taking one step forward. "I don't need you here. And no, I'm not that same sixteen year old girl." I take another step forward as he faces me. My heart is racing. I swear it's never beat like this before. "And to most people, I might stay stuck as that little girl until I'm gray and wrinkled, but I'm not her."

I stop, standing in the middle of the room. My chest rises and falls, yet it feels like there isn't near enough oxygen in the room.

"I don't need you here, Lexington," I say softly. "But I want you here. And that's a first."

He crosses the room in three long strides. His hands slide into my hair, pulling my face to his. And with hunger and truth, I press my lips to his.

My choice.

My decision.

For once.

Finally.

Of what I need. Of what I want.

His lips are firm under mine, his mouth inviting me in. My hands rest on his hips. My entire body gravitates to his, pulling us closer, leaving no space between us for conflict or hesitation.

The weeks of smiles and laughs, the early morning walks and jokes over pizza. The plotting and unsure moves.

They've all easily led us here.

I think I always knew this was where it was going to lead.

I just didn't know how to get here.

"I want to be with you, Elle Ward," Lexington breathes out into my lips. "In whatever this new life is, fighting whatever battles we have to fight. I want to be with you. My fearless woman."

I sigh into his mouth and his hands slide down my back, onto my hips, which I press into his, unable to get quite close enough. My back suddenly bumps into a wall and Lexington's kisses trail from my mouth, to my cheek, to my jawline.

My head falls back, my eyes rolling as electric sparks replace my blood. My hands slide down Lexington's arms, feeling every rise and fall, every definition of every muscle there.

"I want you here," I repeat again. I melt down through the core of the earth as he presses his kisses straight up my throat. I open my eyes, meeting his glowing red ones. But I only pull his face back to mine.

The sharp tips of his fangs graze my tongue as I kiss him. Inhuman strength occupies his hands as he grips my shirt and pulls me closer.

It shouldn't be shocking that I would eventually fall for a vampire someday.

"I'm not going anywhere," Lexington breathes as his kisses slow. He laces his fingers into my hair, studying my face as he pulls away. I stare into his eyes, short of breath, watching as very, very slowly his eyes fade. The red giving way back to their formerly human blue.

"I'm in love with you," I confess.

I thought I'd be scared when I finally made that confession someday, if the day ever actually came.

But I'm not.

"I thought that I shouldn't," he says, tracing his finger down my cheek, along my jaw. "But everything about you makes me. I love you, Elle."

I press my lips to his again. Just letting them be still, letting mine rest against his. Breathing this air between us in and out, sharing the same oxygen.

The grandfather clock dings softly, the time turning over to four in the morning.

"Stay with me tonight?" I ask him quietly. Comfort and ease settle into my system. Something warm and soft. Knowing we're right where we belong.

"No place I'd rather be." His lips brush mine when he speaks, offering promises.

He takes a step away, his hand sliding down into mine. He takes another toward the stairs, pulling me along behind him. He holds my eyes the entire time, as if he's still searching to be sure I want him here.

He hesitates in the hallway between our two bedrooms.

I push the door to my room open, and pull him in behind me.

For the first time ever, I pull a man into my bed with me. Lying on top of the blankets, he extends an arm and I curl myself into his side.

Placing my head on his chest, I hear his Resurrected heart pound. My hand rests against a firm chest, covered by his own hand.

Lexington presses a kiss to the top of my head and I let my eyes slide closed.

Peace rolls through my veins, telling me this is exactly where I want to be.

chapter
TWENTY
TWO

SOFT SINGING FLOATS TO MY ears and even though it grows quieter, its location grows closer. I slit my eyes open just slightly. Lexington walks in through my bedroom door. Utterly silent, he crosses the floor and climbs back into my bed, shaking it very little.

Fingers very lightly trail up and down my spine, moving first over my exposed skin, then over the thin fabric of my undershirt. I keep my eyes closed, smiling to myself as I keep my face toward the door.

"I know you're awake," Lexington says softly with a smile in his voice.

"I know you know," I say, still keeping my eyes closed. "I'm just enjoying this."

Soon his gentle fingers are joined by soft lips and a scratchy beard. He presses a line of kisses across my shoulder blade, working his way from my spine, out to the tip of my shoulder.

I finally turn my face, looking up into his incredible blue eyes.

"Have you ever noticed how our eyes are almost exactly the same shade of blue?" he asks quietly, almost as if he can read my mind.

"Really?" I ask as I reach up and lace my fingers through his wild hair.

"Really," he says as a smile crooks on the left side of his mouth. "Look." He reaches over to the bedside table and grabs his phone. Flipping over so he's on his back, he lies by my side. He pulls up his camera and turns it around so we can see ourselves.

I, of course, notice my wild mane of blonde hair and the flushed nature of my cheeks.

But there's Lexington, smiling up at the camera.

Both of our blue eyes glow brilliantly in the mid-morning sun, shining through the window.

"You're right," I say, looking at the blue. I have a little ring of gray around the outside of my eyes, and Lexington's are slightly brighter, but they are indeed almost the exact same shade of blue.

He snaps a picture unexpectedly and I laugh, and he quickly snaps another of the two of us.

"Stop!" I protest, just as he presses his lips to my temple, snapping yet another.

"I can't!" he says loudly as he tickles my stomach. My nose scrunches as laughter bubbles from my chest and he continues snapping selfies of the two of us. "It's a modern age, and every precious moment must be documented!"

"Lexington!" I squeal as his fingers dig into my side. I'm out of breath, worming my way away from his treacherous fingers. "No one likes to be tickled!"

"But it produces the most adorable crinkles on your nose," he says as I straddle him, my knees resting on either side of the bed on both sides of his hips. He grabs my wrists, smiling up at me.

I lean forward, balancing all of my weight into his hands. Slowly, I bring my nose to his. My hair cascades down around us, casting us in our own cocoon. The smile on his face grows more serious and I see his eyes drift around my face, slowly sinking down, taking all of me in.

The undershirt I wear is thin, exposing the excitement he brings out in me. The jeans I fell asleep in last night are tight, low cut. My bellybutton is exposed, my top pulled up in our wrestling match.

He studies me, so I study him in return. The rise and fall of his chest muscles. The V-neck of his shirt dipping low, giving me a preview of the beauty I know is there. The sharp jawline. The scruff on his face. The tossed state of his hair.

"This is real," I whisper as I bring my lips to his cheek. Softly, I brush them over his skin, letting that reality sink in. "Right here. Right now. This is real."

He turns his face, bringing my lips to his. Gentle. Soft. Understanding.

Somehow I don't doubt that he knows exactly what I'm meaning right now.

"Can I have you?" he whispers into my lips.

I meet his eyes, and suddenly I see everything. The mornings. The days. The evenings, and the nights. Together.

"We've been each other's for weeks already," I tell him the truth as I lean forward, capturing our hands between our chests as I let myself sink into his lips.

Lexington rolls us, propping himself up on an elbow, looking down into my face. "This is different," he says as he brushes a hair behind my ear. "I just need you to know that. Everything with anyone before was always difficult. This... I didn't think these things could happen easy."

I nod. "I hope you realize the different woman you pull out of me. I've never been the most joyful person. But with you... that's just what I feel."

He traces his fingers down my face, trailing down the side of my neck.

I bite my lower lip, trying to put the emotions I've been struggling with for weeks into words. "Everything that happens in our past defines us. All those big and insignificant events. They make you who you are. I just always assumed there was too much darkness in me. It sucked away all the chances at real happiness or joy."

I look up into his eyes. "I just always thought I'd be on my own. I mean, I had Alivia. I had Ian, but he didn't really know me. Not in the important ways. So I just settled that I was enough for me. I just couldn't see myself ever finding someone I fit with."

The look in his eyes, says it all: we just are. We just settle into each other.

"We're total opposites in most ways," I say with a smile. "But you're the one and only person I needed to fill in the rest of who I am."

"If you really think about it, it's a little bit of a miracle we found each other," he says, sliding his hand down to my hip, his palm resting against my bare skin. "Born across the country, a century and a half apart. How many little circumstances had to fall into place at just the right time."

A smile pulls at my lips, and he's right. The impossibility of love has a way of putting everything into place.

I was never the kind of person to believe that until a few weeks ago.

My stomach growls, and my eyes grow wide in embarrassment.

"The woman may be fearless, but she is still human!" Lexington declares. He climbs from the bed, pulling me up as an even bigger smile overtakes my face. "The woman who has taken siege of my heart needs sustenance and so I shall provide!"

"Wait, wait, wait," I say, pulling back as he tries to lead me out of the room. "I feel disgusting. Let me at least change."

"You've got two minutes," he says, pressing a quick kiss to my cheek and ducking into his own room.

I smile happily and slip into my closet.

It's a Sunday. I see snow outside blanketing the ground, at least six inches deep, but the sun shines brilliantly.

It's certainly a day for pajamas. I settle for an oversized nightshirt, pushing the sleeves up to my forearms, and slide on a pair of slippers. A visit to the bathroom, and I pull my hair up into a messy bun on top of my head.

Stepping outside of my room, I hear Lexington shuffling things in the kitchen. Shada darts down the stairs ahead of me, skirting around the corner to go hide somewhere.

When I round into view of the kitchen, I falter, hugging to the wall, feeling my face instantly blush.

Lexington stands at the counter, his back turned to me. All he wears is a pair of red sweatpants.

Giving me full view of all that glorious skin of his.

Suddenly, he looks over his shoulder at me, and I feel my face blush all the harder.

"All those words spoken last night and this morning, trust me, Elle, you have full permission to look as much as you like." His tone is teasing, but also incredibly proud.

I give a tiny squeal, hiding my face in my hands. "This is so…"

"Incredible?" he says, and I hear him step forward. "Wonderful? Fantastic? Perfect? Romantic? I can go on and on."

He gently pulls my hands away from my face, forcing me to look him in the eyes. The smile on his face is without a doubt the most adorable thing I've ever seen.

"Will it make things easier for you if we make this official?" he asks, his eyes dancing. I give him a little nod, playing along. "Elle Ward, will you be my girlfriend? Thus giving you full rights and privileges to look at my naked body any time of day or night. Giving you the right to be bossy and demanding I make chocolate runs whenever the need strikes you. Will you officially be mine?"

I bite my lower lip, trying to contain the most ridiculous smile that has ever been on my face, in all twenty-three of my years on this earth. "Yes, Lexington Dawes, I would be absolutely trilled to officially be your girlfriend."

Oh, how that smile of his kills me.

"Say it," he pleads.

"Say what?" I play dumb, even though I think I know exactly what he wants.

"Say the word," he begs, leaning in closer. "Make my freaking decade. Please say it."

I look into his eyes, reaching up and wrapping my hands behind his neck. "I'm your girlfriend, Lexington. And you're my boyfriend."

A triumphant laugh breaks from his lips just a moment before he wraps his arms around me, crushing me to him as he takes my lips.

As he backs away, taking my hand in his, and pulls me into the kitchen, I ask myself again, for the millionth time, this time for different reasons:

How is this my real life?

The waffle maker is in full demand and we go back and forth with the toppings, getting creative. And things just get crazy and messy when a can of whipped cream is found in the back of the fridge.

"Can I ask?" I say as I step over a splatter of something runny and sticky on the floor. Lexington immediately turns, placing his hands on my hips, the look on his face turning deep and lustful. "Where did you get the scars?"

I raise one of my hands to touch the one on his chest, lightly brushing my fingers over it. My other hand slides to his back, running over the raised scar there.

"You know not everyone made it out of that fight with the Bitten," he says quietly as his eyes study my face. "I just about didn't walk off that field."

Tightness grips my chest, choking the air from my lungs. I bite my lower lip to hold in the sorrow that sweeps over me. I didn't know it then, but on the worst day of my life, I almost lost the man I would come to love someday.

"It's okay, Elle," he says, bringing his hand up to my chin, drawing my eyes back up to his. "I'm still here, and I like to think stronger for it."

I put on a little smile and nod. "What about the tattoos?" I ask, trying to move on from such a dark memory.

Lexington turns slightly, looking over his shoulder toward the three tattoos that occupy his shoulder blade. "They're the years my siblings were born. I kind of started feeling like I was forgetting them, it was such a long time ago. Now I carry them around with me always."

"That's beautiful," I say quietly, leaning in and pressing my lips to his.

Knowing Lexington, I should have anticipated him grabbing the whip cream and suddenly sliding the tip between our lips and giving it a big squirt.

Twenty minutes later, licking a glob of peanut butter from the back of my hand, I go to the fridge for some milk. I grab a bag of blood while I'm in there, handing it off to Lexington while I pour myself a drink.

"I know this sounds absolutely disgusting to you," he says as he opens it. "But mixing this blood into the batter sounds amazing right now."

And for a second, the thought does turn my stomach. But with a smile, I take the bag from him, and pour half of the O+ into the batter. I hold his eyes with a tiny smile as I mix it in.

"And I'm absolutely done for," Lexington says, wrapping his arms around my middle and burying his face into my neck.

It's absolutely unorthodox. There's nothing normal about the way I feel his fangs graze over my skin as he kisses his way from my shoulder up my neck. Or the ultra strong grip he has on my nightgown, pulling it up my thigh.

Nothing natural about the blood waffles I make for the one and only boyfriend I've ever had. Nothing casual about this house we live in with two-dozen poisonous plants buried beneath the snow on the roof.

But it's my version of absolute perfection.

chapter
TWENTY
THREE

"Come on come on come on," Lexington coaxes the car as we attempt to make it up the slight hill to the House. It snowed again last night, bringing another four inches. It's nearly a foot deep at this point.

"It's been hours since they plowed," I say, looking down at the road. It's covered in a thick sheet of snow and ice. "Everyone is at home with their families."

"We got this," he says, putting the car in reverse and backing down the hill to level ground. "I grew up in New England, I will not be bested by snow and a hill!" He gives a war cry, pressing down on the gas, rocking us forward.

A squeal rips from my throat as we slip for a moment, but we're climbing. And finally, we make it up and crest the hill.

"Yeah, baby!" Lexington cries triumphantly, pumping his fist in the air as he turns right and parks in front of the House.

Lights twinkle from inside, barely still detectable in the early afternoon light. Lexington and I grab the packages in the back seat and hurry inside, letting ourselves in.

"Oh, wow," I say as soon as I step foot inside.

"And I'm instantly starving," Lexington says as he takes my coat, hanging it on the coat rack behind the door.

It smells amazing inside. Turkey and potatoes, some kind of pie. Memories of cooking Thanksgiving dinner with Lula flood through me instantly.

And the rest of the house is decorated classily. A huge tree dominates the living room. Wreaths and glittering deer and garlands are splashed throughout the house, adorned with red and white ribbon.

"You made it through the snow." Julie walks around the corner, a warm smile on her face. She practically glows, and instantly I know who did the decorating.

"Wasn't going to let just a little bit of snow keep me from celebrating Christmas," Lexington says jovially as he leans forward, kissing Julie's cheek. But he keeps my hand in his, pulling me along with him.

"Is it Christmas?" a dark voice calls from within the house. Michael rounds the corner, an annoyed look in his eyes. "I hadn't realized."

"Michael," I greet him, looking him up and down. He's dressed similarly as the other night. Jeans, boots, a denim coat. He's combed his hair back and cleaned his beard up a little bit. "How are you settling in?"

His expression darkens and he looks around, taking in the festive decorations. "It's been an adjustment."

I crack a tiny smile for him. It's comical, really, seeing him in this setting after our last encounter.

"You can put the presents by the tree," Julie says as Duncan steps out into view. His eyes instantly drop to me and Lexington's hands, which are still clasped together.

"No more agony?" he asks as a smile grows on his lips.

"We both got what we wanted," I say, flashing a little smile.

"Guess that means you're finally off the market," Aleah says, giving me a dark look, even though a coy smile curls on her lips. "The eternal bachelor has been claimed?"

"That's right, gentlemen," Lexington says loudly. "She's mine. Don't touch. Don't even look at her or I'll have your throats."

Except I know he's all talk. He's not like that. Possessive is the opposite of everything he is.

"Yeah, yeah, the love birds are here to rub their happiness in our faces." Robert walks down the stairs, brushing past us without so much as a look in our direction.

I look around as everyone gathers in the living room. Eva, Julie, Robert, Michael, and Duncan. Kai is absent, and I'm glad he's spending the holiday with his family.

It's obvious from the stiff and formal conversations that all the members of the House of Martials are having that they're still getting used to each other. Most of them have only been together for a few days now.

I don't know if it's their common curse, being what they are. But their kind does seem to bond quickly. They form relationships, families.

I watched it happen in Alivia's House. And I'm sure it will happen here, given time.

But I just feel like an outsider.

I don't need mass amounts of friends, a huge family.

I just need a few people in my life who mean a great deal.

It's hard to imagine myself fitting in with these people. I never did back in Silent Bend.

But looking over at Lexington, who laughs at some joke Duncan made, who does fit in with these other vampires so well, I know I'm willing to try.

Six Born vampires, and one Bitten, sitting around a tree on Christmas morning, laughing, telling stories. Some of them are recent. Some from fifty years ago. Some from over a hundred.

Wrapping paper forms a big pile in one corner of the room. Duncan receives six new books, a new briefcase from Julie, and an ugly sweater with a reindeer on it from Aleah. Aleah gets a lot of new black clothes. Eva receives several cookbooks and a huge wok. Apparently she's the one who's been cooking the delicious smelling meal.

Michael gets a pair of socks from Julie and a bag full of my glass orbs filled with vampire acids from me.

I give Duncan a look, and he offers a smile before darting up the stairs. He comes back down a minute later, carrying a huge box wrapped in silver paper.

"Whoa," Lexington says with a huge smile as Duncan sets it down in front of him. "What's going on with this?"

I feel my face flush red. "It's from me. Open it."

All eyes turn to Lexington as he gets this little boy smile on his face, clearly thrilled to be receiving anything. He rips the paper, pulling open the box.

And a reverent look comes over his face as he pulls the guitar case out, and opens the lid.

"Is this…" he breathes, running his fingers down the neck of the guitar. "Is this what I think it is?"

He looks over at me, his eyes dancing with excitement and wonder. I nod, unable to contain the smile. "It is."

"Is what what?" Michael asks. He leans forward in his seat, craning his neck to get a better look at what rests in the case.

"A 1968 Fender Strat," Lexington says in awe as he lifts the white guitar from its case, setting the case on the ground. He shifts the guitar so it rests on his leg, the neck in his left hand. He plucks out a string of chords, testing it out. "It's the same guitar Jimi Hendrix played at Woodstock. Same…same white color and everything."

"Are you telling me you were at Woodstock?" Michael asks with amusement and respect. "*The* Woodstock?"

"Hell yes I was," Lexington says with a laugh. His fingers fly over the chords, plucking out some kind of song. He's actually good. Like, impressively so. "Crazy, crazy scene. Amazing. But crazy."

"You sure you want to be in a relationship with this old fart?" Robert says. "He's practically ancient, and what are you, eighteen?"

"I'm twenty-three," I say sharply, quickly growing tired of the assumptions.

"Elle," Lexington says, looking up at me with wonder. "This...this is amazing. Like, literally the most perfect gift anyone has ever gotten me, or ever will get me." He leans forward, pulling my mouth to his. "Thank you," he says against my lips.

"You're welcome," I say, blushing, because every one of the other six people in the room is watching us. PDA is a first for me.

"You better have something pretty impressive after what she just pulled off," Eva says with a smile. She sits on the floor, her ankles crossed, her forearms hanging over he knees.

"Well, Elle certainly has put me to shame," Lexington says. He sets the guitar in its case, though he leaves the lid open. "But I hope this will be adequate."

He hands me a bag. A huge one that is seriously heavy.

I look up at Lexington as I pull a layer of tissue paper off the top. He watches me with nervous, excited anticipation, and my heart does a little fluttering backflip.

He's called me adorable before, but Lexington is pretty damn adorable too sometimes.

The first item I pull from the bag is a pair of gloves. Black and silky. Next comes a hat and then a pair of thick, wool socks.

Item after item, I pull out a coat, thermal underwear, footie pajamas that have little skulls all over them. And finally, an electric blanket.

"What is all that crap?" Aleah asks with a condescending laugh.

"I'm always freezing," I laugh, buried beneath a mountain of things to keep me warm.

"You've obviously never felt this woman's feet," Lexington chuckles, pride shining in his eyes at everything he's bought. "They're like ice cubes, all the time."

"You guys are so cute," Julie says with a smile.

I laugh, handing the cord over to Duncan so he can plug the blanket in for me.

"And that's not all," Lexington says as he cocks an eyebrow at me. He disappears for a moment, the front door letting in the tiniest draft as he goes in and out. Almost instantly he appears back at my side, holding something out with a paper bag over the top of it.

I look up at his eyes with a little smile, excitement and just a little anxiety fluttering in my chest.

I'm really not someone who likes surprises.

I pull the bag up, and my face freezes in wonder.

A single stem rises up from a planter pot. White flowers with yellow centers jut out all around it, the petals frayed and fringed looking.

"Is that a fringed prairie orchid?" I ask in awe as I take the pot from Lexington's hands.

"Sure is," he says with pride.

"What's the big deal about an ugly flower?" Eva asks.

"They're getting to be really, really rare," I explain as I look it over, searching for stress or damage to the plant. "They're about a dozen plants away from being on the endangered list."

I look up at Lexington, awe in my expression. I want to ask how he got it, but I can just see how happy he is at my reaction to his gift.

So instead I just lean forward, and press my lips to his. "Thank you," I breathe.

"Gag me," Aleah says. I look over to see her roll her eyes, slouching deep into her chair.

Everyone else laughs, and I've had enough PDA for now.

"Dinner is ready," Eva says, providing a thankful distraction.

"Let's eat," Michael says as he jumps to his feet. "I'm starved."

The presents now all opened, the clock reading noon, everyone files into the dining room. A long table dominates the room, a dozen chairs set up around it. Everyone pitches in, taking the food from the ovens and refrigerator to the table. Julie smiles admiringly at the beautiful table setting she's laid out.

And for just a moment, as everyone dishes up their Christmas dinner feast, I forget that these people are anything but that.

Until Robert breaks out the enormous pitcher full of thick, red liquid. One by one, he makes his way around the table, filling the wine glasses with blood. Until he reaches me, giving me a wink, and skipping over me to fill Lexington's cup.

"This is wonderful, Eva," I say as I near the end of my plate. "Did you go to cooking school?"

She nods from the end of the table, next to Aleah. "I was in New

York, just two weeks away from finishing it up."

"What happened?" I ask as I take a sip of my cranberry juice.

"Nine-eleven," she says. "I was right under the building when the towers came down. I was pulled from the rubble two days later and woke up in a refrigerated box two days after that."

"That's terrible," I say, my brows furrowing. "Did you know before?"

She shakes her head.

So many like her never knew what they were before they died and Resurrected.

"What about you, Julie?" I ask.

"You could say my mother was obsessed with vampires," she says with a laugh. "She always loved folk lore, scary tales. So when she learned vampires were real, she hunted one down. Slept with him, much to the threat of her physical safety. Nine months later, I was born. Twenty-seven years after that, she convinced me to take my own life and see what would happen."

"Wow," I say. Her mother doesn't sound much better than mine.

"How did the two of you meet?" I ask, looking from Julie to Eva.

"I just smelled her," Eva says. "I know it sounds weird, and you probably can't understand as a human, but we can tell." Each of the other vampires nods. "We were both in Baltimore at the time. Neither of us had met another vampire."

"We've been keeping an eye on each other ever since," Julie says, offering a little smile to Eva.

It's hard to imagine the two of them being friends naturally. But when they thought they were the only ones, what other choice did they have? They needed someone who understood what the other was going through.

And somehow along the way they met Michael.

I understand now why they joined the House so readily. The promise of others like them, with the possibility of meeting many more? It must have sounded incredible.

Eva has just started cutting up pie when there's a knock on the door.

I climb to my feet to get it, but Duncan jumps up. I follow him toward the front door.

"A package for Miss Elle Ward."

Shock and dread jolt my system like I've just stuck my finger in an outlet.

The voice behind Duncan is shaky, full of fear. Duncan steps to the side slightly, and I gain line of sight.

A man in his mid-thirties stands on the front porch. His entire body trembles in fear. And on the right side of his neck are two puncture wounds with trails of blood leaking from them.

"There's no one here by that name, sorry," Duncan says, furrowing his brows in confusion.

Lexington suddenly darts to the door. "I'll take that," he says. He steps through the door, looking in either direction up and down the street. "Who sent you?" he asks the man quietly.

"I…I can't…" the man says, emotion breaking his voice. "They have my family."

Lexington puts a hand on the man's shoulder. "I understand. You've done your job. Go home."

The man bites his lower lip and nods his head. Hardly able to walk, he's still trembling so bad, he makes his way down the stairs.

"Who's Elle Ward?" Duncan asks as Lexington turns. His blue eyes meet mine, and I see red burning like embers in them.

"What's in it?" I ask as we walk back into the kitchen. He sets the package on the counter and grabs a knife to cut it open.

Lexington opens the flaps, and swears as he looks inside.

I grab the box, pulling it to me, and look inside.

Two dolls rest inside. One in the likeness of a beautiful woman with fiery orange hair, a tiny crown atop her head, wearing a beautiful dress. The other has blonde hair, fragile features, and wears the very same black pants and red and white polka dotted shirt I wear now.

It looks just like me.

I reach inside and pick them up. But the moment I do, both their heads fall from their shoulders, attached to the bodies by a piece of yarn.

Chelsea was killed by my mother. I never saw the carnage, but was told stories much later. Chelsea's head was beaten in, and then decapitated.

I hold the two dolls up, watching as both our heads swing.

"That's dark," Aleah says. I look up to see her watching the heads. "Even for our kind."

Michael crosses to the counter, grabbing the box. He looks down inside. "*A sister for a sister.* What's that supposed to mean?"

He tips the box, displaying the words that are written at the bottom in thick, black marker.

Lexington yanks it away, staring at the words. "Damn it!" he bellows, crushing it to the ground. His hands come up to fist in his hair, his eyes wild and violently red. "I should have known he wasn't going to let this go. Charles is a patient man. He's just been biding his time."

I look back at the dolls, my head now resting still, unattached from my body.

He's been spying on me. Today. In the last few hours.

"You talking about the Allaway prick?" Michael asks, his voice growing dark. "A sister for a sister. What the hell does this girl have to do with his twin sister getting killed?"

I meet Lexington's eyes, and see the fear and the resolution there. It's time. We have to tell them the truth.

"My mother murdered her, and most of his House," I say, still looking at Lexington. "And my name isn't Penny Jones."

"Elle Ward," Duncan says as understanding creeps into his voice. "Ward. That's someone from the House of Conrath. You're..."

"Alivia Conrath is my sister-in-law," I say, looking over at him. "My brother, Ian Ward is married to the House regent. The Battle of the Bitten that initiated the genocide decree? It was my own mother who led them."

More than a few curse words are let loose. The look in Michael's eyes deepens, conflict rising there. Robert looks utterly shocked. Julie and Eva don't seem to understand the history or know what all this means.

"So you're saying she's a direct target of the House of Allaway?" Aleah says. "A sister for a sister? Charles' sister Chelsea, for Ian Ward's sister, Elle?"

"That's exactly what we're saying," Lexington says. He stands there, frozen, his eyes fixed on me, like he's afraid if he looks away, Charles will magically snatch me away into thin air.

I look away, unable to take the agony in his eyes. "We didn't tell you who I was at first because we had to be careful. My brother visited with Charles two months ago. He made a direct threat to me."

"Then why hasn't your brother just lopped the prick's head off yet?" Michael asks with a growl as the yellow lights in his eyes.

"Killing Royals is a big deal," Lexington breathes. He slowly walks in a small circle, the gears in his head spinning faster and faster. "If the House of Conrath takes out the leader of the House of Allaway, it's a declaration of war. King Cyrus likes to deal with these kinds of issues himself. But he's never quick about it."

"Being thousands of years old will do that," Aleah says.

"What an asshat," Julie says with a look of disgust. "You're just trying to help him. That's what all this is about, right?" She waves her hand in a circle, indicating all the people in this house. "And he's coming after you, threatening your life, when you're doing something that will keep him from getting killed by this King?"

"Charles doesn't always think logically," Lexington says. He finally stills, lying his hands flat on the counter top. "He and Chelsea killed their own mother when they wanted the power. Chelsea thought it was entertaining to torture people, and Charles always went along with whatever his sister wanted. To him, all he's seeing is the revenge."

I walk to the dining table and sink into a chair, looking down at the dolls.

What are my options right now?

Run and hide. That's always the method everyone has always suggested to me. Disappear, head to some unexpected corner of the world. There are billions of people on this planet and it's huge. Charles can only look in so many places.

Fake my own death. Take on a new identity. Dye and cut my hair and dress totally different.

Every option leaves me having to say goodbye to the life here that I've fought so hard for.

This feels like a losing battle, one I'm not sure how to overcome.

Footsteps cross the kitchen and Lexington squats down in front of me, his face coming into view. He pulls the dolls out of my hands and sets them to the side. He takes each of my hands in his and my eyes finally rise up to meet his.

"I'm not sure what to do right now, Elle," he says quietly. "I know you don't want to run, and I don't want you to have to do that either."

"Move her into this House," Robert says, though the tone of his voice says he doesn't like the idea. "If we're all here, that makes eight vampires to keep an eye on her at all times."

"But this isn't going to be resolved in just a few simple weeks," I say, looking over at them all. Their willingness to jump to Robert's suggestion is there in all of their eyes. "Charles is an immortal. He has eternity to execute his revenge."

"Then the only option is to kill him," Michael says. His brows furrow, his expression rolling into a gnarled mess of anger. "I don't care if this King comes after me. I'm no one, I can disappear. I'll go kill Charles myself, problem solved."

I look at Lexington's face as he studies Michael. He's seriously considering the plan.

"Is there any chance of reasoning with him?" I ask, pulling Lexington's eyes back to mine. "Would Charles listen if you talked to him? If I talked to him? Would he hear anyone out?"

Wistfulness fills his eyes, but there's also resignation there, too. "This is a family feud now. The Allaways are descendants of the third son, just like Alivia. To them, family is something you fight for. And Charles is nuts."

"You don't have to have this on your conscience, darlin'," Michael says. Suddenly he disappears. I hear footsteps upstairs, loud noises as he shuffles around, and the next moment he reappears, next to the doorway.

His flail hangs over his shoulder. "Just don't ask where I'm going and this isn't on you."

He looks back at me, sincerity in his mad, wild eyes, just a moment before he pulls the door open, grabs a pair of sun goggles from the table next to it, and disappears out into the afternoon sun.

"How much of a chance does he stand against this guy?" Eva asks as she stands at the counter, her hands braced on it.

"They're both totally nuts," Duncan says as he crosses to the front door and closes it, squinting against the sunlight. "So I'd say it will be a pretty evenly matched fight."

"He's going to have to surprise Charles," Aleah says, crossing her arms over her chest. "Michael may be crazy and a good fighter, but he's still only a Bitten. Charles is a Born, and his House may be small, but he still has some followers."

I swallow, my eyes falling to the floor.

I've only known Michael for a few days, but already I've found myself feeling very fond of him. His loyalty. His hot reactions. His readiness for change and plans.

No wonder Alivia is so affectionate toward Markov.

If he gets himself killed trying to help me…

I close my eyes and shake my head. I can't think like that right now.

"If he does kill Charles," I say, looking back up at Lexington. "What will happen? To those who follow him? To his House and title?"

"Some of you probably don't know this, since you've never met the man," Lexington says, looking up at our own little House. "But Charles is gay. I've watched him run through a parade of lovers over the past thirty years. He's never produced an heir. Neither did Chelsea before she Resurrected. They're the end of the Allaway line."

Lexington stands, crossing his arms over his chest. "If Charles dies, King Cyrus is going to have to instate a new family to rule over our region."

"Who?" I ask, shaking my head.

Lexington shrugs. "I don't know. Isn't everyone who lives back at Court in *Roter Himmel* a Royal? Maybe someone from there would be willing."

I nod. In my time in *Roter Himmel*, I learned a lot. Located in Austria, it's a town full of vampires and humans alike. Each of the vampires is a direct descendant of the third or seventh son, and thus, Royal. But they don't rule

Houses there. They're just ordinary citizens, though considered members of Court. Their motivation for living there is that they don't have to hide what they are. They have an agreement with the humans. They feed as needed on the human population, and take care of them financially in exchange. It's a peaceful town, and they don't have to hide their basic nature.

"Maybe," I say. My head is spinning.

If a new Royal family is instated, it means King Cyrus will likely come to the North East. It means more of his twisted games.

"Well, I guess we better buckle up for a rocky ride," Aleah says, stabbing a fork into the pumpkin pie on the counter.

"And until we get word from Michael that Charles is dead, I think Robert is right. You need to stay here," Julie says, resting a supportive hand on my arm.

Defeat sinks in my chest. "Okay." I nod.

But when Lexington looks into my eyes, he knows the truth of what I'm feeling.

I haven't had to hide in four and a half years. Haven't had to have vampires protect me against other vampires. I've been able to protect myself for this long.

And here I am again, back to what it was like when I was sixteen. When I was two years old.

The fragile human, threatened by a set of fangs.

"We'll get through this," Lexington says softly as he reaches out and takes my hand in his. "Just give it time, and I promise you'll get your normal life back."

TWENTY FOUR

WE DON'T EVEN DARE LET anyone run back to my house to get any of my things. If Charles tracked me down to the House, how likely is it he won't figure out where my home is?

So I'm stranded at the House without any of my things. Without my cat. Without my garden. None of my clothes. Nothing familiar or comforting.

The holiday weekend rolls by. No word from Michael.

On Tuesday, Lexington, Robert, Eva, and Aleah accompany me to Oleander Apothecary. Charles already knows where that is. I gather some of my things from there, take as much work stuff as I can, and load it into Lexington's car.

Just before I'm about to leave, I notice the light for the room downstairs is on. But when we go to check it out, there's no one there.

Someone came looking for help, and I was locked up, being watched over.

Some poor soul is probably going to live out the rest of their days as a vampire when they don't want to, and I could have helped them if this wasn't the reality of my life.

No matter how hard I try to fight it.

Before we leave the shop, I hang a sign up in the window: *Closed until further notice.*

I think of all the customers who come to me on a frequent basis. All the people I help, all those who turn to me when everyone else has failed them.

And now I have my hands tied.

Lexington reaches over and takes my hand in his as we drive back to the House. I feel his eyes on me, but I can't bring myself to look up at him.

Numbness starts creeping into my chest, and I fully welcome it.

As a stand-in House, we discuss if we should tell the House of Conrath what has happened. In the end, we decide not to. I know the second Ian hears there's been face-to-face threats, he'll be at Charles door, driving a stake through his chest, putting himself in the line of danger.

And this is what we're trying to accomplish in this House. We need to figure out how to deal with our own problems. This is the job of a House. We'll figure out a way to solve this.

Four days later and we still haven't heard anything from Michael.

I won't say it out loud, but I'm pretty sure he's dead.

He's tough. He's cunning. He's loud and confident.

But despite the fact that it isn't his fault, that he can't do anything to change it, he is still only a Bitten. Going up against an enemy that is so much stronger than he is.

I stand at the window a week after Christmas, staring outside as snow gently falls. It's nearly dark, but light glows from the street lamps. Cars drive by outside, on their way about their normal, mundane lives.

I hate them all right now.

"You hungry?"

I don't turn to see Lexington when he walks into the bedroom that used to be Michael's. I hear him close the door behind him and walk half way across the room.

"No," I answer simply.

A woman walks down the sidewalk, her heavy boots making prints in the slushy snow that sticks to the sidewalk.

I want nothing more than to trade places with her.

"Elle, you have to keep eating," Lexington's voice comes nearer. I feel the heat of his body against my back, and he places his hands on my upper arms. "I've seen you take two bites of every other meal in the past week. I'm worried about you."

"I'm fine," I say emptily.

"No, you're not," he whispers, his lips brushing my hair over my ear. "You're shutting down. You're starving yourself. And this is the Elle I remember as a girl."

"I guess we'll just always be one and the same," I say, letting my vision glaze over, not seeing anything anymore. "I thought I could change it all. But our destiny always finds us."

"Don't call an enemy destiny," Lexington says, pulling me around so I face him. I look up in his eyes, not feeling anything. "This is not some grand scheme, Elle. This is a maniac doing something to you that you don't deserve. Don't give him cosmic credit."

"Maybe it's just punishment," I say. "A delayed reaction for my past sins."

"What are you talking about?" Lexington asks. He lets his hands slide down, taking mine in his.

"Six years ago I shot and killed my own mother," I say, remembering the smell of the rifle. How I struggled to figure out how to load the bullets. The blood that covered my shoes as I walked through a field of slain Bitten. "I didn't even consider another option when I knew what she'd done. When I learned the truth. I murdered the woman who gave birth to me. There has to be some kind of repercussion for a heinous act like that."

"Hey," he says, his voice growing desperate. He grabs my chin and forces me to look at him. "Don't give up on me. Don't drown right now. I saw you do it, Elle. I watched you sob, fat, big ol' tears that rolled down your cheeks when you pulled the trigger. You're still a human being, Elle. Don't let that go."

But I want to. Emotions are simply too draining for someone like me. I'd rather empty out.

"Please look at me," Lexington begs. And maybe I'm not empty enough, because the emotion in his voice compels me to do so. "We're going to make it through this. You've lived through a lot of other shit, and you're going to make it through this, too. And when it's all over, we're going to go back to meandering walks through this city, eating at random pizza places, laughing about the stupid things I did back in the sixties."

Something in my chest tries to put a smile on my face. But it doesn't quite have enough energy.

"Don't give up," he says, his eyes brimming with desperation. "I need you, Elle. I love you."

And that echoes true. That reaches down in my soul, grabbing onto the drowning woman who's already slipped under the surface, taking hold of the two fingers that are still barely above water.

"I love you, too," I say, and my voice cracks.

And then my chest cracks.

All of me fractures.

I let myself fall into Lexington's arms, and shatter to pieces.

Chapter TWENTY FIVE

"Pretty sure that's the second time he's looped our block," Eva says as she peers out the curtains. I work at the kitchen island, pouring the last of the toxins into the vials. Boxes surround me, brand new supplies, which is frustrating, since I have everything I could possibly need back at the shop. But I can't go back and get them. The kitchen is a mess, my supplies strewn all over the place.

But I have to keep myself busy.

It's been six more days of lock up and I'm getting stir crazy.

"It is," Robert says, twirling a stake in his hand, shifting to the side of the door, looking out into the dim gray evening. "But he never looked at the house."

"Doesn't mean he isn't casing the place," Eva says, her eyes following whomever it is outside.

"Do you really have to do that here?" Aleah asks grumpily as she walks out of her bedroom and takes in the state of the kitchen. "I mean, from what I hear, that stuff will take every single one of us down. Doesn't it seem kind of rude, making it in front of all of us?"

"She has to do something," Duncan counters her. He's been sitting at the bar this entire time, watching and observing as I combine my ingredients, putting them through different processes. "What if something happens to us somehow? How do you think she's defended herself for the past few years?"

"The least you could do is clean up," Aleah says, still trying to sound annoyed, but losing her steam.

"I'm almost finished," I say, corking the vials. I check the needle caps, making sure they're all in place as they should be.

"I think we should call Lexington and let him know," Eva says, still looking out the windows.

"You know he's not going to be thinking clearly about if the man is guilty or not, right?" Robert says. He finally seems satisfied the suspicious man is gone, and steps back away from the window. "That's exactly what he did with the last one."

Robert is right. Two days ago, Lexington caught someone trying to sneak onto the fire escape on the second floor. He barreled out the window like a man possessed, eyes red, stake in hand. He had the man pinned to the pavement on the ground outside in two seconds. The very briefest flashes of red shone in his eyes for just half a second before Lexington staked him through the heart.

He's on edge. Ready to do anything.

"Kai or Julie, then," Eva says, pulling out her phone. She talks quietly into it, describing the man, giving instructions to follow him for a bit and then question him. A quick confirmation, and she hangs up.

"So, is it the castor bean that is the active ingredient?" Duncan asks while I take all of my tools to the sink, putting the rest of my supplies into a box.

"Castor beans contain ricin which is deadly, even in small amounts," I explain as I load the beakers and measuring tools into the dishwasher. "One or two seeds could kill an adult in less than ten seconds. Even just a tiny amount of it can cause severe vomiting, seizures. But no, it's not the castor beans that are the active ingredient."

"Then the white snakeroot?" he asks. He's been asking a million questions all night.

"I'll never tell," I say, a small smile on my lips as I rinse the saucepan out. "If I told you, I'd have to kill you, right?"

Duncan laughs, shaking his head. "You're an interesting person, Elle Ward. I didn't think people who knew plants and roots like you do still existed. Once upon a time, everyone probably would have called you a pagan or a witch doctor."

"I'm okay with that," I say as I throw in some dish soap and start the washer.

"So tell me, why *Oleander* Apothecary?" I turn to face Duncan, who studies me through narrowed eyes. "It looks like an innocent enough flower. Is it just ironic?"

"Oleanders are seemingly innocuous," I explain as I place the fresh new batch of toxins in a container. "But every part of the plant is deadly. It contains lethal cardiac glycosides known as oleandrin and nerline. If you ate any part of an oleander plant, it could cause vomiting, erratic pulse, seizures, coma. Even death."

Duncan's eyes widen, but a smile pulls at his lips and he shakes his head.

"Even just touching the leaves or the sap can cause skin irritation." I smile as I see the understanding take Duncan over as I explain the surprising truth about oleanders. "The toxins in oleanders are so strong that people can even become sick after eating honey made by bees that visited the flowers."

"Then why do so many people grow such a deadly plant for decoration?" Duncan asks with a chuckle.

"Thankfully it tastes awful, and who really wants to eat part of an oleander?" A smile pulls in one corner of my mouth.

Duncan laughs out loud, tipping his head back. "Okay, I get it now. Beautiful, seemingly innocent, but deadly when you get down to the root of it. Oleander Apothecary is … the perfect name."

The front door opens and Lexington walks in. The moment his eyes lay on me, a brilliant smile pulls on his lips.

"There's something I haven't seen in a while," he says, locking the door behind him. "Whoever got her to smile, keep doing whatever you're doing."

"Wasn't really me," Duncan says, looking back to me. "Just get her talking about toxic plants, something a little dark and sinister. Seems to do the trick."

"I will keep that in mind," Lexington says as he walks up to my side. He presses a kiss to my temple, his hand coming to the small of my back. "Duncan, you're up."

Duncan swivels on his chair. He heads to the stash of weapons by the back door and gears up with stakes, toxins, and even a handgun.

"Still no word from Michael?" Lexington asks as he looks around the house to those guarding me.

"Nope," Aleah says, and the tone of her voice says it. She thinks he's dead, too.

Lexington's lips press into a thin line, and he doesn't seem to have anything to say about that.

"Do we all need to consider going after him?" Aleah says. "Besides me and you and Duncan, the House of Allaway doesn't know the rest of us. We might be able to take him out."

"I can't let you all take a risk like that," I say, shaking my head. "We have no idea what happened to Michael, I can't let that happen to anyone else."

"I'm just saying, it might be a good long while that you're stuck here," she says, raising her eyebrow.

"I'll think of something," I say, stacking the box of toxins on top of the box of supplies and yanking them from the counter with too much force. Glass rattles around inside.

Without another word to any of them, I head for the stairs and walk up to my temporary bedroom. Lexington's footsteps follow me and he closes the door behind us. I set the box on the dresser and stand with my hands braced on it.

"Elle," he says, walking up behind me.

"I'm fine," I cut in. "Really. I'm sick of being here, sick of not knowing anything. But I'm okay. I have to be, because the alternative is to keep feeling like this and I just don't have the energy for that."

"Okay then," he says, accepting my words without any questioning. It's not surprised. Not doubtful. Not mocking.

I turn, sitting on the edge of the dresser, facing Lexington. I reach out, grabbing the lapels of his jacket, my eyes studying his chest. I feel his eyes on me, but I just study his body.

"I think we could both use a little distraction," he says quietly, huskiness settling into his voice.

I pull his jacket back over his shoulders, letting it slide down and drop to the floor. One of his hands comes to the side of my head, his fingers lacing back and into my hair. I pull the cardigan I wear off, the cool winter air hitting my bare shoulders, my camisole thin.

"We're going to get to be happy again," I say as I let my fingers slide along the hem of his shirt. Silently, I let them slip beneath, the tips of my fingers touching warm, hard skin. "Those few days before Christmas, they were just a preview, right?"

Lexington lowers his face, his lips making contact at the space between my neck and shoulder. His facial hair tickles, sending currents of sparks racing through my blood. "On a tiny, little fraction of what is to come, Elle."

I stand, letting my hands rise as I do, running up and over his stomach, up to his chest. With one smooth movement, I raise his shirt over his head, freeing him of it.

Still, I don't meet his eyes. I let my own study his chest, the valleys and peaks of his stomach muscles. The jagged scar that cuts across his left breast. The two little freckles under the right one.

I bring my hands back to his skin, running them smoothly over him. Goosebumps flash over my own as his hands come to either of my sides, skin to skin as he works his thumbs under my top.

"I want a million more moments like this," he breathes as he brings his lips to the corner of my mouth. He brushes them over my flesh and my muscles go weak and my head lolls to one side. "Five hundred thousand nights. Five hundred thousand mornings waking up beside you. Seven million opportunities to hold you."

My eyes slide open, finally searching out his. They're brilliant in intensity, showing me the truth of every confession. My hands slide up from his chest to either side of his neck.

Slowly, studying his every feature the entire time, I pull his face down to mine. Slowly, I breathe the air he breathes.

When our lips meet, they're warm and soft. They mesh together as if they were designed from the beginning of time to belong to one another. My hand slides up, wrapping in his hair, my entire arm curling around his head so he can't escape. His hands slide down to my hips, gripping them firmly. He pulls my body closer to his and more electrical sparks go off in my veins.

Bad things happen to us. People do us wrong. Lives are threatened.

But this life will still be my choice. I will claim every moment. Doing everything I can to still be Elle Ward.

Fearless.

Strong.

And in this moment, right here, I choose to be happy. Wrapped in the arms of an immortal man who fell for a mortal, fragile girl.

I choose this.

chapter
TWENTY
SIX

"IT'S REALLY IMPORTANT YOU MEASURE everything accurately," I say as Lexington hands me the vitamin A and E. "Any imbalance and this stuff will dry you out or make you really oily."

"Got it," Julie says as she double checks the lanolin. "I just want it exactly like that batch you gave me at Christmas."

I offer her a little smile, stirring the oils on the stove, apricot, almond, coconut, and beeswax.

"What's this stuff called again?" Lexington asks as he walks back to his laptop which sits at the island. He sits down, tapping away at the keyboard.

"Perfect Me," I say as I turn to measure the aloe vera gel.

"It really is perfect," Julie says with a smile as she watches the oils begin to thicken. The color turns creamy. "My skin has never looked so amazing."

Lexington chuckles and shakes his head, his fingers flying over the computer.

He's been putting all of his hacker skills into trying to dig up anything on Charles Allaway. And so far there's been nothing. Charles has been a ghost lately.

I pull out the lavender essential oil. Dropping four drops into the blender, I turn it on low and add the rest of the ingredients.

"You want it to be the texture of buttercream," I tell Julie, showing her the way it grows fluffy and white. "Usually takes just two minutes. See? It's just…about…there."

I shut the blender off and Julie claps her hands excitedly. I can't help but smile a little as she slides over the glass jars and scoops the cream into them.

"Thank you," she says as she dips her finger in the still fluffy cream and rubs a small bit onto her cheek. "I'll get all this cleaned up."

"Thanks," I smile, stepping aside to let her finish. I pull one of Lexington's hands away from the computer, dragging him after me into the sitting room, staring out the window.

I don't have many supplies right now, despite the constant parade of boxes I've had delivered to the House. I'm finding it's the only way I can remain sane while on lock down, when I haven't left the House in two full weeks. Not even one toe outside the door.

"I'm worried about Shada," I say, watching the snow gently fall outside, a thin coat of it covering the streets of Cambridge. "I'm sure she got into the bag of food, but she's probably running low by now."

Lexington sits at my feet, tracing patterns into my socked foot. It takes everything I've got to not flinch away from the tickle.

"Everyone except Julie and Duncan are out on patrol right now," he says, resting his chin on my knee and looking up at me in a very adorable way. "It's been pretty quiet, though I think we learned our lesson about letting our guard down. But maybe I could dart over there real fast and get her."

"Really?" I ask hopefully. I feel my entire face light up, and didn't realize just how much I've missed the dismissive feline until now.

Lexington chuckles, shaking his head. "What I wouldn't do to see you smile like that all the time."

Heat flushes my face, but I don't care. Lexington rises to his knees, wedging himself between my knees, and leans forward to kiss me.

"Is she going to claw me to death the second I pick her up, though?" he asks against my lips, and a laugh bubbles from my chest.

"Possibly, but I think you're a little tougher than most," I tease him, pressing one more quick kiss. "She has a carrier in the laundry room."

Lexington pushes himself up to his feet and gathers some supplies. Fully armed, he heads for the door, me following behind him. I push my hands into my pockets, leaning against the wall.

"I should be back in thirty minutes," he says, looking over his shoulder.

"Thank you," I say, my chest glowing with the truth of the words. "I love you."

The smile he offers could melt me into a puddle. "I love you, too."

With a wink, he closes the door behind him, and he's off on the rescue mission.

"You sure have him wrapped around your little finger," Julie says, walking out, waggling her eyebrows.

I only blush hard and laugh.

I head up to my room where I open up a new book I got this morning and curl up into the bed.

It's a historical tale, set in the colonial era of the States. Full of damsels in distress and muscular heroes who have a tendency to lose their shirts.

The sound of the door being kicked in rocks through the house. There's a yell and feet pounding before I can even leap to my own feet. I grab my blow dart from the bedside table when I hear the sound of what I'm afraid is a body hitting the floor.

I yank my door open, ready to fight with every bone in me, when I stop short, nearly plowing into a body standing there.

"Hello, Elle Ward."

Lips curl into a smile. Freckles line a face crinkled with a wide smile. Fiery red hair dances in the afternoon light.

"Charles," I breathe. He steps forward, forcing me to take an equal step backward. I bring the blow dart up to my lips, but before I can fire, he swings up a cell phone.

"Uh uh uh," he says, waving a finger back and forth. "I suggest you not."

My eyes focus on the screen of his phone, and I immediately recognize the broad shouldered man who walks in through the front door of my house.

Lexington.

"You had someone follow him," I say as all the adrenaline raging through my system turns cold.

"You lot here may be doing some good work, but you really don't understand how politics and a vendetta work," Charles says while my eyes continue to study the streaming video of slight movement inside my house. "Me and my remaining House members have been here in Boston for a month now. Watching. Learning. Waiting."

My eyes widen and flick up to meet his. They aren't quite green, not quite blue. And they're full of pride in finally having caught me.

"Julie and Duncan?" I ask. The house is silent, save for the sound of two sets of feet walking around.

"They're in quite a lot of pain right now, I do believe," Charles says, and one side of his face curls up in a smile. "You have quite the interesting selection in that little shop of yours. Some very sinister creations coming from one so fragile."

My eyes darken and my fingers roll into fists. "What do you want, Charles? If you're here to kill me, leave Lexington out of this, and give it a try."

Charles laughs, a barking and startling thing. "Oh, so much spunk! You are certainly not the little mouse brought to be judge at *Roter Himmel*!"

My heart pounds and my mind is racing. I could try to take Charles out, but if he doesn't give word to whoever is following Lexington, he could and I'm sure will, get hurt. Or worse.

I'm not left with many options.

All because I missed my stupid cat.

"Don't try to logic your way out of this one," Charles says with a smile. He begins a circle around me, reaching out and running a single finger through my hair, brushing it over my shoulder as he makes a track around. "You're going to cooperate with me, and from the looks of it, we need to hurry."

He holds up the phone again, and I see Lexington lock up my house, the cat carrier in one hand.

"What do you need me to do?" I ask as I swallow, my eyes fixed on the screen as the spy follows Lexington down the block.

"You'll follow me out to the vehicle waiting in front of this house, and you'll not cause a problem on the little drive ahead of us." Charles stops in front of me again, looking very smug and satisfied. "If that is too difficult, well, Harrington carries quite a big blade with him, and it has been known to sever bone and spinal cord."

"Let's go," I say immediately. I set my blowgun on the dresser and walk past Charles, who bears a look of surprise on his face.

"You said we need to hurry," I say, as I look back up the stairs to where Charles stalls in shock. "We better get moving."

In the living room, next to the Christmas tree, convulses Julie, her eyes squeezed closed in agony. Duncan lies face down in the hallway, one of his hands outstretched toward me. He looks at me, anger and regret and death in his eyes, but he's completely immobilized.

Two women and one man stand waiting in the hallway, wearing sun goggles.

Without another word, I push aside the door that hangs broken on its hinges and step outside. A black SUV waits across the street.

"Let's go," I call back to the crew that hesitates in the doorway, costing us precious moments before Lexington returns home and gets himself killed because he's outnumbered.

One of the women climbs into the drivers seat, and I let myself into the back seat. Sliding to one side, Charles sits beside me, the man in the very back, and the other woman taking shotgun. Each of them fiddles with their sun goggles, making sure they're securely in place against the harsh light.

"I'd appreciate it if you hurried," I say calmly. "There's no reason to make a scene, and I don't think it will take Lexington very long to get back."

Charles chuckles, though it sounds uncomfortable. "You heard the woman."

We pull forward, and I hear the doors automatically lock.

Down the road we roll, toward the mess of freeways that stretch all throughout the Boston metropolitan area.

"I must say, I didn't expect this to be so easy," Charles says, not quite looking at me.

"It doesn't have to end in dramatics that just get more people killed," I say, staring out the window, and never once granting Charles the pleasure of making eye contact. "You're here for me. Not anyone else. A sister for a sister is easy enough to understand."

He's quiet for a long few minutes, and I feel him studying me. We cut through town, and then pull onto a freeway, the one to head northwest, up toward Vermont, I'm sure.

"Why aren't you afraid?" Charles asks finally.

I take a deep breath, looking out at the city that begins to fall behind me, turning into a new one. "I think I've been waiting for my death since I was two years old. In the world I've always lived in, it was just expected that the end would come too early."

He doesn't respond, but I feel his eyes continue to study me.

I know very little about the House of Allaway. Just that it is located somewhere in Vermont. That Charles now rules it on his own. That it's small in numbers.

And Charles is supposed to be a spastic nut job.

Ten minutes into the drive, my phone starts ringing. I pull it out to see a call from Lexington, the phone displaying a picture of him. Charles rips the phone from my hands and throws it out the window.

As we cut down freeway after freeway, it's hard to find any comparisons between this man and Alivia and Henry, the only other Royal Born I know.

Alivia exudes leadership and grace. She's sure and confident, she knows how to get people to love and follow her. Henry is the definition of a Royal. The way he holds himself. The legends he's created.

Charles, on the other hand…he just seems weak. He seems juvenile. Despite the fact that he's led a House far longer than Alivia has.

The members of the House of Allaway speak a little here and there over the course of the next two and a half hours. We cross state borders into New Hampshire, and then into Vermont.

The sky grows darker as we pull off the freeway and start down a narrow highway. Cutting through hills and gorges, over bridges and between a million trees that have long since lost their leaves, and evergreens that stand as shadows in the dark, we drive.

We pass through a small town fifteen minutes after pulling onto the highway. For another ten minutes we drive through more trees, the night growing darker by the second as the sun falls behind the horizon.

Finally, I spot a sign on the side of the road, welcoming us to Woodson, Vermont.

A few little shops pop up here and there, another stretch of trees, and then we seem to hit town. It's a short strip of the highway, dotted with old buildings that look like they were built in the early eighteen hundreds. A library, city hall, two churches.

There's certainly some history to this town.

Just before we reach the end of the shops, we turn north, onto a small and narrow road. We drive for ten minutes, heading into dense trees and up a hill.

Finally, so deep into the woods you'd never have hope of finding it unless you knew exactly where it was, a huge house comes into view.

Rock walls rise high and wide, a mix somewhere between a stone cottage in the woods, and a castle. Our vehicle pulls to the left and rounds into a garage.

"Come," Charles says, offering a hand to assist me. Everything in me recoils as I take it, stepping out of the vehicle.

He leads us through the garage and to a door that opens inside. When we step through, we enter a mudroom, which cuts into a kitchen that's beautiful and grand, but still reasonable. From there I can see a dining room. Charles cuts to the right, and the woman behind me shoves me forward. I follow behind him and we enter into a great room.

A huge fireplace dominates one wall and comfortable, overstuffed furniture is spread throughout the large space. Big windows are scattered along the wall to my left, though it's pitch black outside and I can't see a thing out there.

The house certainly is nice and comfortable. Big and well taken care of. But it's not what I pictured when I imagined the House of Allaway.

"You'd better hurry and get killing me over with," I say as I look around. Everything seems too new, too…unused. "Because this is the very first place Lexington is going to come looking for me. I wouldn't call this a good hiding place."

"This is the perfect hiding place," Charles says with a coy smile curling on his lips. "Because this isn't the House of Allaway, and your irritating boyfriend has never been here before. We're still some distance from the official House."

Cold adrenaline burns down through my veins.

I didn't see that one coming.

And the smug smile on Charles face tells me it's obvious on my face.

"Throughout the years, many of the Houses have established secret, secondary Houses, in case they ever needed escape from the official residence. Chelsea and I picked this one out together, about nine years ago, and until today, none of my other House members have been here."

That explains why the four of them are looking around the place like they've never seen it before today.

"Lexington, your brother, and your sister-in-law might come looking for you, but they'll never find you out here," Charles says with that creepy smile of his.

I raise my chin just slightly. "What does it matter anyway, you're just going to kill me and send my head back to Ian."

A low chuckle bubbles up from Charles' chest. The glint in his eyes darkens. "Oh, I do plan to have your head, but I have other devices to execute first."

He nods his head toward the stairs, which lead down, and both of the women grab my arms, shoving me toward them as we follow Charles.

Darkness steals my vision as we walk down them, until finally, a few lights here and there grant enough to make out a hazy picture as my eyes adjust.

The center of the space is finished roughly. There sits a couch and two chairs, a fully stocked bar off to the side. Along one side is a row of doors with windows looking into them, on the other side, another similar row.

Straight forward is a narrow row of windows, each of them covered in steel bars.

"So you're just going to keep me prisoner here?" I ask, faking unimpressed when really I'm doing everything I can to keep my heart rate under control.

"No, my darling," Charles says, his smile growing. "It's going to be a little more complicated than that."

"Aw, shit." A familiar voice calls from behind one of the doors. My eyes strain through the dark, and through one of the barred openings,

Michael's face appears. His hands grip the bars, resting his forehead against them. "He finally caught up to you."

"Michael?" I gasp, taking a step toward him, but one of Charles' women grabs my arms with a vice grip. "Have…have you been here the whole time?"

"I knew eventually that fool Lexington would let down his guard, and once I brought you here, I figured you would like some company," Charles says as he walks to the bar. He pours himself a drink, and raises it up to his lips, staring at me over the edge of his glass.

"You shouldn't be here, Elle," Michael says, and the look in his eyes tells me he knows something. "This isn't going to be good."

"I'll do the talking, lumberjack," Charles spits at him.

"Oh, but I highly doubt you're going to tell the whole story," Michael taunts, that smile of his curling on his face. "Elle, make sure you ask him about the part that involves his impending death in the next year."

"That's enough!" Charles bellows. He hurls his glass at Michael's cell, shattering the glass just inches from his face.

Instantly, Michael's eyes turn yellow and he bares his fangs with a roar.

"You may as well tell me what's going on," I say, folding my arms over my chest. "It sounds like I'm here for the foreseeable future, so I'm good with a long story."

Charles's red eyes glare at Michael, but slowly slide over to me.

"The House of Allaway is an old one, generation after generation reproducing and then killing their predecessor if they don't agree with the way things are run. Father and child, creating an established rule."

Some cold creature is spawned in my lower belly. I feel it send shots out to every part of my body, the muscles in my face growing weak.

"The death of my sister has brought to my attention the weakness of our family," Charles says, but there's something hesitant there, uncomfortable, in the tone of his voice. "I need an heir."

"Tell her the truth, Charles," Michael taunts, his expression somewhere between disdain and a smile. "Tell her what good ol' Cyrus told you."

Charles' expression grows sour, and he very much looks like he'd prefer to kill Michael rather than let him live to keep me company.

"Word has gotten to Cyrus that my House is weakened," Charles says, still staring death at Michael. "He's not happy."

"Keep going, *Lord* Allaway," Michael growls when Charles stalls.

"The event of my death could happen at any time, just like any of us," Charles says, turning away from Michael to return to the bar. "Establishing a new family to reign is an inconvenience to the King, but he also doesn't care for the way I've been running things on my own."

He pours another drink, this one filled to the brim. He doesn't raise it to his lips though, he simply stares into the depths of the dark liquid. "King Cyrus commanded I produce an heir within the next year, or he'll replace me."

I swallow hard, a chill running down my spine.

By replace, Cyrus means he will kill Charles. And let another family take over the North East Atlantic area.

"If I produce an heir, he'll let me live until the child is old enough to take over, and perhaps give me a chance to redeem myself in his sight."

243

Charles brings the glass to his lips and tips his head back, downing all of the contents.

He growls, smacking his lips and dragging the back of his sleeve over his mouth.

"I think most of the world is aware of my...preferences, when it comes to partners in my bed," he says with a little chuckle. He finally turns, and he seems to grow as whatever plan he's come up with sits just under the surface, waiting to be revealed. "Producing an heir is a more complicated matter for the likes of me."

The cold in my body spreads to my hands as they go numb. I feel my eyes widen. Dread begins clawing it's way up my stomach.

"But thankfully, modern medical practices make this a much more pleasant experience for me, rather than having to go against my nature." The smile curls on his lips.

A door opens behind me, and a man steps out, wearing a lab coat, a grim expression on his face.

"I told you this was gonna' be bad, Elle," Michael says in a low voice, looking at me with so much regret in his voice.

I swallow again, but my mouth is dry. My hands begin to tremble just slightly. "What are you saying, Charles?"

The smile on his face can only be described as evil. He crosses his hands in front of him, his stance wide and cocky. "I'm saying, with the help of Dr. Gethrow here, we're going to conceive an heir."

My entire body feels numb. I can't move. Can't breathe.

"I'm saying, we're going to artificially inseminate you, and you, Elle

Ward, enemy of my House, will pay for the sins of your family with your body," Charles says as his voice grows low and quiet. "You are going to carry and give birth to my heir. And when the child is born, I will cut off your head, and have it delivered to the front steps of the House of Conrath."

A small sound slips past my lips, a squeak or a cry. But I'm absolutely frozen.

"Damn you, Charles," Michael hisses, his eyes glowing brilliantly through the dim space. "You sick, twisted bastard. May you burn in hell for this."

"Perhaps," Charles says with an amused smile as he looks back over his shoulder at him. "Little is known about the afterlife for vampires. Hell, heaven, limbo, nothing at all. Thankfully my kind gets a very, very long life before we have to worry about it."

My hands flutter to my stomach, and I look down at it.

This is a nightmare. This can't be real.

"Dr. Gethrow," Charles says. "How about we get started? Time is of the essence."

The two women grab me roughly once more and drag me toward the room the doctor stepped from.

Suddenly the breath rips in and out of my chest in harsh gasps. My eyes wildly search for an escape route, for any way to fight back.

"Elle!" Michael yells, reaching through the bars toward me. "I'm sorry!"

I'm pushed over the threshold into the room.

In horror, I look around.

A stainless steel table sits in the middle of the room. Leather straps are affixed to the sides of it—restraints. Around the room are countertops with various equipment on them. Needles and microscopes.

It's a fully stocked lab.

"No," I breathe, shaking my head as my eyes go wide. "No, please!"

"A sister for a sister," Charles chuckles as he follows us inside. The two women bruise my arms as they shove me onto the table, pressing my head back as the doctor straps me down. "But first, you shall help ensure my immortality."

"Please," I beg as the first tears spring into my eyes and break free. "Don't do this."

But the door closes, and Charles locks us all inside.

THE END OF BOOK SIX

about KEARY TAYLOR

Keary Taylor is the *USA Today* bestselling author of over a dozen novels. She grew up along the foothills of the Rocky Mountains where she started creating imaginary worlds and daring characters who always fell in love. She now splits her time between a tiny island in the Pacific Northwest and Utah, with her husband and their two children. She continues to have an overactive imagination that frequently keeps her up at night.

To learn more about Keary and her
writing process, please visit: www.KearyTaylor.com.

Made in the
USA
Columbia, SC